Solitude Lake

By Adele Darcy

Firehole Press

Printed in the United States of America

Firehole Press

ISBN: 979-8-218-00469-9

Table of Contents

Chapter 1

Susan Dixon lost herself in the frozen scenery of Solitude Lake. Thick fog obscured the formidable, craggy peaks of the Swan Range. Snow pounded fiercely as the wind howled like a Yeti. The thermostat on the Lone Moose cabin porch hovered at thirty-eight degrees.

"Spring is a hostage to Jack Frost." Susan shivered, content to be lost in the loneliness of the storm. Spring in Montana was a time of extreme conflict, as new life struggled to emerge from the iron fist of winter.

Her heart ached as she glanced at the calendar: May 1. Left a widow at the age of thirty-seven, Susan had endured a grueling six months. Losing a loved one can break the spine; it cracks the heart and sucks the air from the lungs.

In the months following her husband's death, Susan's moods had contorted violently between abrupt surges of anger, where she lashed out in a thunderous rage, and an interregnum, where she relented. She'd give up the ghost for a second, cleansing her senses in a flood of tears. The cycle repeated as the pain swelled up again, then iced back over into a state of frozen bitterness and desolation.

It was fitting that spring in the Northern Rockies was known as the "the mud season." Every ounce of Susan's frame, flesh, and spirit felt the grime and filth of soiled mud. If life was a journey, she navigated its wilderness in a state of confusion. The soiled memories and harsh unknowns like graves in sand. Susan had lit a frayed wick of bittersweet hope to strain her compass back to the place she'd once called home: Solitude Lake.

For Susan, Solitude Lake had once evoked a sense of peace and tranquility. It was her safe place. Today, the lake was anything but tranquil as a winter tempest thrashed outside.

This land was at war with the elements. In the past week alone, two feet of snow had pummeled neighboring Solitude Peak before a warm front breathed life into the mountains. The vacillating weather, triggered a series of backcountry avalanches that shot down the canyons.

Nearby, Hidden Creek and the Swan River were in the throes of ice jams, causing isolated flooding. The metamorphosis of seasons was a painful transition as winter relinquished its cold crown, yielding to the dynamic beauty of summer. The result was a summer of heaven on earth, but in the interim, the general situation was a miserable existence.

Solitude: Susan pondered the word. It was the state of being alone. Susan had never felt more alone in her life. Solitude, a detachment from civilization, remoteness from habitations, or generally a lonely unfrequented place. Deserted, empty, isolated… Those words described the landscape and inner conflict in her soul.

In the middle of the storm, a patch of blue sky emerged, revealing the rocky apex of Solitude Peak.

Susan stared into the heart of the mountain. The coarse sawtooth pike coming out of the mist like a guardian spirit. Its alpine splendor inviting wild hearts into its mystery and magnificence, while also warning souls not to tread too close. It was a dangerous beauty.

The mountain's Morrell Glacier, a tundra left over from the last ice age, reminded Susan it would take more than a flash of sun to melt the frozen fort she'd built around her soul.

December 13

6:53 p.m.

Susan pulled into the driveway at her five-bedroom Victorian she owned with her husband, Bradley, in Seattle's Queen Anne district.

She had fallen in love with the property during a historic tour of the neighborhood. When it went on the market a few weeks later, it seemed out of reach. Somehow, Bradley had managed to come up with the financing.

7:00 p.m.

Susan unloaded the car. It was cluttered with Christmas gifts, including the Angel Tree toys for the Salvation Army Drive, and a "North Pole" special surprise for her husband.

She had toiled for months searching for the perfect gift. Bradley was easy enough to please—, but she wanted to give him something special.

While perusing the Spellbound Used Bookstore in Pike Place Market, she'd been fortunate enough to stumble across a first edition of Charles Dickens's classic *Great Expectations*.

Well worn, the book was stained, with oiled pages, obvious damage from the wear and tear of years of constant reading. Susan wondered how such a well-loved book had ended up here, in an off-the-beaten-path used bookstore.

The owner was obviously not a connoisseur of the market. Susan understood Dickens's first editions were apt to fetch upwards of several thousand dollars at auction. Then again, the dismal wear and tear of the hundred-and-fifty-year-old parchment and binding made it a forgotten gem, an orphan of sorts to fend for itself. Susan purchased the edition for four hundred dollars. Charles Dickens was a mutual favorite of the couple. Bradley would adore the gift.

7:15 p.m.

Susan called Bradley's cell phone to check in with him at work. It went straight to voicemail. *He must be on a job.* His position as owner of a construction firm routinely forced him into sixteen-hour shifts. It wasn't uncommon for Brad to come home late—sometimes he'd crawl into bed after midnight.

7:20 p.m.

Her stomach grumbling, Susan decided to order takeout from the neighborhood Chinese restaurant. Brad would appreciate the leftovers when he got home.

8:42 p.m.

Susan stepped into a steaming hot shower.

8:53 p.m.

Her cell phone rang five times before Susan answered, towel still in her hair. She didn't recognize the number, but hoped it was Brad calling from a jobsite.

"Mrs. Dixon?" The heavy, unfamiliar voice at the other end of the line spoke in an ominous tone. "This is Detective Mike Mallicote with the Seattle Police Department."

"Detective, how can I help you?" Susan asked, perplexed by the call.

"I'm sorry to tell you that your husband was involved in a serious car accident on I-5. The ambulance arrived on the scene within minutes. The paramedics did everything they could to revive your husband…"

"Is Bradley injured?" Panic set in.

"I can only offer my condolences. Your husband did not survive the accident."

Susan collapsed on the cold hardwood floor, speechless. Shock hit her like a silent thunderbolt.

"The road was wet," the officer prefaced.

"Seattle is always wet," Susan argued.

"Brad hydroplaned," he continued.

"He's a good driver," she countered, still in denial. Bradley was too young to be dead.

"He swerved, barely missed a car in the neighboring lane, only to crash into the median. His car caught fire, leading to a small explosion."

"Oh God, why?" Susan's last gasp of denial was caught up in images of fire, rain, and death. A piece of her soul was missing. "God, why? How could this happen?" She gripped the cross necklace Bradley had given her so tightly it almost broke.

In the week following Bradley's accident, the medical examiner phoned Susan with details of the autopsy report.

"The deceased died on impact. He felt no pain, dying instantly from severe trauma." The examiner's tone was procedural, almost sterile, as he consistently referred to her husband as "the deceased." The doctor meant well but lacked the personality to convey compassion deeper than medical jargon.

"By the deceased, you mean my husband, Bradley Dixon," she uttered into the receiver. The information from the medical examiner did not console Susan. It only cemented the fact that her beloved husband was dead at the age of thirty-eight.

They'd had plans and adventures ahead of them. Christmas in Seattle, and a New Year's Eve ski trip at Snoqualmie. Then there was the trip to Greece in March to celebrate their seventeenth wedding anniversary. Summer at Solitude Lake in the cabin… Susan would have to reconcile those losses as forgotten memories.

The pain that stabbed like a rusted nail was the loss of their chance to have a child together. For years, they'd struggled to start a family, due to Susan's infertility caused by polycystic ovarian syndrome. Although Susan and Bradley understood you didn't have to have children to reflect the strength of one's love, they both longed for the chance..

It was a slap in the face that something as mundane as driving home from work could explode into catastrophe. An instant in traffic abruptly ended a life, and nearly destroyed Susan's as well.

She was haunted. Grief, anguish, rage, turbulence, fear, and sorrow weighing her down.

If not for her strong Christian faith, the grief of losing him would have smothered her. There had to be some hope in suffering. Some understanding in sorrow. The loss of Bradley had stolen her peace. She had to pick up the pieces.

Chapter 2

Cozying up by the fire, Susan found consolation looking over family photo albums at the Montana summers that had molded her youth.

Susan grew up in Hidden Creek, Montana. It was a small idyllic town nestled in the picturesque Swan Valley, fifteen miles north of Condon and thirty miles south of Bigfork on Montana Highway 83 in the northwestern corner of the state.

Formed by the colossal forces of glaciers, erosion, and the uplift of the Rocky Mountains, the Swan Valley was a true gem amidst the many natural wonders that the Treasure State had to offer.

Straddled by the steep snowcapped Swans to the east and the towering Mission Mountains to the west, the adjacent Swan and Clearwater Valleys were defined by lush, dense forests of ancient larch and cedar, lodge pole and aspen. More akin to the coastal forests of the Cascades in Washington and Oregon than the high plains and fire-prone hills east of the divide, the Flathead National Forest in the Swan District was home to a diverse mix of flora and fauna, including a healthy population of grizzly and black bears, elk, deer, mountain goats, and moose.

The region was nicknamed the *lake corridor*. Glacial activity ten thousand years ago had formed over two hundred lakes in the vicinity. Hidden Creek boasted three lakes within five miles of the town's parameters: Solitude, Mystic, and Kokanee Lakes. That didn't include the over two dozen lakes located in the neighboring backcountry or within a twenty-minute drive.

Hidden Creek took its namesake from a small stream that held significance to the Kootenai tribe that used to call this land home. The town was founded in 1898, when amateur geologist Emmett Belton, betting on gold in the area, began a mining operation on the creek banks. It didn't take long for the prospect to realize that the only gold in Hidden Creek was the blue-ribbon trout.

Emmett shifted his focus from mining ore to tourism and logging. He advertised the Western frontier and romanticism of the lakes, organizing backpacking, fishing, and hunting expeditions.

In addition to his tourism empire, Belton established the Willow Flats Logging Company, which used surprisingly advanced forestry practices at the time.

Today Hidden Creek had a population of 978 year-round residents. The population swelled to 1,600 in the summer months when summer people left the hustle and bustle of city life for the tranquility that the wilderness can provide.

Susan's great-grandfather Ned Blanchard, an architect hailing from North Carolina, fell in love with the region while on a backpacking trip in Glacier National Park in the 1920s. On a whim, he acquired five acres of land on the south shore of Solitude Lake, where he built the Lone Moose This rustic, charming cabin had served as the Blanchard family's summer home for over ninety years.

Ned was a storyteller at heart. He could craft and weave words into tales of heartfelt suspense, fantasy, drama, and intrigue. During his campfire sessions," he recounted stories of Solitude Lake's mystical powers. He claimed the lake's waters had the power to heal the broken in spirit. The folk stories, a mix of Native American legend and Ned's creativity, were passed down to Susan through her father, Doctor Kip Blanchard.

After finishing medical school at Vanderbilt, Kip had moved his wife and daughter to Hidden Creek permanently. The town needed a doctor, and he desired the haunting beauty that only the lakes region could offer.

Since Brad's death, Susan's thoughts often turned to her father's sage advice. She pondered how Kip Blanchard would handle the mess that her life had become. He would tell her to let go of the anger. *Easier said than done.* Susan gritted her teeth. Kip would remind her to keep fighting the good fight. "Look at Solitude Lake—you can drown in your sorrows or start kicking and swimming to the other side…"

Doctor Kip Blanchard was a loving father, doting husband, and renowned medic, who at the drop of a hat personally sacrificed his own livelihood for others in need. He was a friend to all, exercising compassion, giving dignity to the least.

A conservationist at heart, Doctor Kip was also a self-proclaimed protector of the forests."

With thousands of acres of dense forests, Hidden Creek was central to Montana's timber industry. These forests were habitats for an interconnected ecosystem of the great grizzly down to the teeniest pika. Kip was an advocate of sustainable logging to strengthen the vitality of the forest, preventing forest fires and improving the local economy through utilization of resources. What Kip Blanchard opposed was haphazard policy that would scar the land in the name of greed.

He ran for a seat in the Montana legislature on the platform of protecting a virgin section of Hidden Creek Flats Forest from a Bureau of Land Management logging contract. In the heart and heat of the contentious logging fight, Kip died without warning from heart failure.

For Susan and her mother, Beatrix, Kip Blanchard's death stopped their world from turning. Time dangled by an instant and everything changed in a span of seconds.

"Funny." Susan managed a cynical smile. The pain of losing her father was nothing compared to the deep, irreparable wounds that Bradley Dixon's death had inflicted on her. She knew her father had been a good man and was in a better place. There was a tenuous peace in that conviction.

She could not find peace in Bradley's absence. The aftermath of her husband's death had unearthed cruel hidden secrets. Bradley had a dark nature she'd been blind to.

Susan met Bradley Daly Dixon the summer of her father's death, while working at the Solitude Lake Lodge, alongside Jake Arnett... But that was another story.

The irony of their friendship and eventual love was the fact that Bradley was the son of Ellis Dixon, the reclamation specialist that Kip Blanchard abhorred. Ellis Dixon's family had strong political ties in the state capital of Helena, which he flaunted at every twist and turn.

Born to homesteaders in Eastern Montana, Ellis Dixon made his fortune in the oil fields in Texas before returning home. He settled in Butte, where he fell in love with Elana Daly, a distant relation to Copper King Marcus Daly. Elana had inherited a significant sum of shares from her father's mining company.

While Elana was known for her beauty and grace, Ellis Dixon was the definition of cutthroat. He resorted to bribery, trickery, and any means of disregard for humanity to get what he wanted. Ellis was a brutal husband and a worse father.

The Dixon family moved to Hidden Creek when Bradley was seven. His father had invested in a lumber company and wanted to log in a protected area of the Flathead Forest. Ellis began his lumber operation in Hidden Creek Flats, which threatened to contaminate the creek and hurt the forest.

The battle over Ellis's logging business divided the community of Hidden Creek. Those dependent on logging for their living felt that conservationists were ruining their livelihood, while others viewed Hidden Flats as a sacred place that should be protected, not only due to the unique ecosystem the forest possessed, but also the fact that the alpine wood wasn't ideal for logging.

Susan's dad led the charge against Ellis's lumber business. Kip Blanchard was able to convince the Montana legislature to set aside the area as protected land. Ellis Dixon was given another lumber deal outside the area as a symbol of goodwill.

Ellis Dixon, never one to lose a fight, held a grudge against the Blanchards and spat on her father's grave when he died.

Elana Dixon opted to divorce her husband and settle in Hidden Creek. She purchased a large lakeside property on popular Mystic Lake.

Bradley had always been at odds with his father. He battled the internal conflict of wanting to please his father's every whim versus rebelling against him entirely.

In retrospect, perhaps that had motivated Bradley to court Susan. It was the perfect way to take a dig at his father…all the while holding power over a creature who in her younger years was so fragile. At least, that was how Bradley referred to Susan during their courtship, "a fragile wingless bird" that he'd rescued.

Susan knew now that she'd never needed Bradley to rescue her. If anything, she'd been his crutch. It turned out that he was the fragile, broken one. What she thought was love now seemed like a game, a project to fix all the problems in a broken girl only to break her wings again when she least expected it.

Susan had struggled with her weight through middle and early high school. Standing just under six feet with broad shoulders, she was naturally muscular, which made her the ideal athlete. Growing up on the water, she became known as the "mermaid of the mountain," serving as captain of the swim team. Still peers made fun of her stature. She was big compared to the lanky and gangly girls who attended Missoula Prep, the private school her mother insisted she attend for academic excellence. Susan had little self-esteem and had struggled with eating disorders. Through competitive swimming and medical treatment for PCOS, by her seventeenth birthday she'd lost fifty pounds and her acne had cleared up.

Bradley on the other hand was the sort of handsome that made girls instantly weak in the knees. He exuded charm. He was confident without being arrogant. A letterman in basketball, he received athletic scholarship offers from across the Pacific Northwest. Never in a million years did Susan Blanchard think that a guy like Bradley Dixon would fall for her—then again, maybe he never did.

The month after Bradley's funeral, estate attorney Johnston Parker had requested that Susan come to his office for a reading of the will, as well as a discussion of other estate issues.

Susan had been so consumed by the grieving process that she hadn't worried much about the estate. She didn't expect a large inheritance as much as for the estate to be fiscally solvent and the finances to be intact enough that she could continue with her daily existence. With their house paid for and a decent joint retirement fund, even without Brad's salary, she could get by comfortably on her salary as an elementary school teacher.

"It's good to see you again," Johnston said when Susan arrived at his office "My wife and I are keeping you in our thoughts and prayers."

"Thank you. It's been a slow process," Susan responded. "You said that you need to discuss urgent matters related to the estate?"

"I wish I had better news." Johnston hesitated. "I regret that your husband has placed me in an extremely difficult position. I always respected Bradley, but what he's done to you is cruel and vicious."

"I don't understand." The words *cruel* and *vicious* did not match Susan's definition of her husband.

"This is going to come as a complete and utter shock…" Johnson let out a hard sigh. "Not only did your husband disinherit you, his financial records show that he also looted $400,000 from your IRA."

"Brad would never do that," Susan dismissed. "He always ensured that our finances were secure."

"The fact is that Bradley Dixon betrayed you. He's been stealing money from your IRA fund for years."

"I don't believe you." Susan's gut twisted. "Why would he go behind my back?"

"Bad investments mostly. He needed capital to pump into the construction business. It seems that he had a gambling problem as well."

"If his business was suffering, he could have come to me directly," Susan argued. "Or we could have taken out a small-business loan…"

"Brad took out plenty of loans," Johnson scoffed. "Over a million dollars in high-interest loans to be exact. He also took out a second mortgage on your house."

"You're mistaken. We paid off our mortgage last June. Also, as co-owner of the home, Brad couldn't have signed off on any additional home loans without my consent."

"Brad tricked you."

"What are you telling me exactly?" Susan asked, unable to deny the cold hard truth that had blindsided her.

"Over the past five years, Brad accrued significant debt, driven by a series of failed developmental deals and bad investments. When he defaulted on several loans, in an act of selfish desperation, he started to empty your retirement account. Determined to hide his fraud, he doctored your financial reports to show that you were increasing your retirement through monthly deposits."

"Are you saying that my savings are gone?"

"Bradley stole every dime from your retirement, except for a paltry $10,000. With your home mortgage paid off, he refinanced the house to the approved capacity. Your current mortgage is $3,000 per month, three years into the fifteen-year loan."

"I cannot afford a $3,000 monthly mortgage on my salary." Susan panicked, feeling the toxic shock of betrayal. Most of her savings had come from her inheritance and investments.

"You have several options. You can rent out the house to help pay the mortgage. Rental income will be approximately $3250 for your house, but you'll be forced to find another housing option, which would run $2000 bare minimum for a one-bedroom apartment or studio in an expensive market like Seattle."

"This is insane," Susan said, struggling to put words to her emotions.

"The second, more viable option is that you put your house on the market. Given the ideal location and the historic character of the home, the house should net an offer quickly. You won't get much from the sale of the house, but with a little luck you won't owe anything on it either."

"We worked so hard to get the mortgage paid off...and now you're telling me that if I don't pay $3,000 per month, then I'm forced out on the street? I cannot reconcile this. Brad had money. He inherited a trust from his grandfather Daly's estate. He ran a successful business..."

"The Daly trust was established in stock shares with the now-defunct Montana Mining Corporation." Parker pulled out the account file. "When Bradley cashed the shares six years ago, they only amounted to several thousand dollars."

Susan shrugged her shoulders. Bradley never went into details about the trust except that it was set aside for their retirement.

"In the early years of Dixon Construction, Bradley made a killing," Johnston continued. "Then he started gambling, gnawing away at company profits. This prompted several unwise business decisions. Add in the housing crash and the Great Recession...the money dried up, while Bradley's debts continued to increase exponentially."

"You said that Brad had other debts, in addition to the mortgage?"

"Brad was wise enough to take out an insurance policy with each of the bank loans, which covers most of his business debt. I was fortunate enough to find a buyer for Dixon Construction. From the company sale, you'll pocket $10,000 in profit. Despite all the financial damage Brad did, you at least will have some funds to tide you over for the next year, $20,000 in cash as of now."

"Just as I'm trying to rebuild my life after the death of my husband, I discover that he disinherited me and ran up a million dollars in debt. Surely the courts can rectify this?"

"Usually, I would advise a court case, in which you as a wife have legal rights to contest the fact you were not listed in the will. However, I think Brad left you out as a blessing. If you were listed, any funds left in his account would become yours, making you liable for his mistakes."

"How sweet of Brad to think of me," Susan snapped. "Either way, he's broken my heart and wrecked my life. How could I be so blind to his fraud?"

"There is one ray of light in this dark tunnel. The Lone Moose, your family cabin in Montana...the deed is in your name only. You own it outright and therefore it cannot be entered into probate as an asset in Bradley's estate."

"I should hope not! My great-grandfather Ned built that house over ninety years ago."

"My advice is that you sell the Queen Anne and move into the cabin at Solitude Lake. It might not be much, but it is a roof over your head."

"I can't quit my job. It's the only source of income to keep me afloat."

"For the record, I spoke with the principal at Hidden Creek High School. They need an English teacher starting next semester and you fit the bill for the job. A change of scenery would do you good."

"Hidden Creek is where I fell in love with Brad. It's hardly a change of scenery."

"Think it over, will you?"

Bradley's deception had thrust his widow into an irreversible financial crisis. Near-destitution did not afford her the luxury of time to think. Mulling over a plan of action would further drain her bank account and lead her to the brink of bankruptcy. If this was sink or swim, she intended to cross the shore kicking and screaming; barely breathing but alive.

Chapter 3

Fueled by adrenaline, Susan sprang into action. Anger and grief would have to wait.

Susan contacted a financial advisor at First West Bank to engineer a plan that would protect her remaining assets and rebuild her retirement. During their meeting at the downtown branch, the financial advisor made it clear that Susan had a rocky road ahead.

"What your husband did to you is incomprehensible. His negligence has severely set you back in your retirement planning. Securing your future will not be an easy process," advisor Tina Romero said, blunt in her assessment. "It won't be an impossible task either. You will have to live frugally."

"What are my options if I want to keep my house?"

"Refinancing is not an option at this point. I've calculated your set monthly expenses…mortgage, insurance, electric, heat, garbage, and other miscellaneous bills that as a homeowner you are responsible for. I also computed the short list of necessary living expenses such as food costs, healthcare, and transportation."

Susan grimaced as the long list of bills piled up.

"To retain ownership of your current home it is going to take working two or three jobs to increase your income. In addition to working extra jobs, you'll have to rent out your spare bedrooms to a tenant or two. The added income will help you keep your home, but you will be strapped financially."

"Incidentals such as a morning coffee stop, a matinee movie, or a pedicure would be off-limits. Your disposable income would be consumed by bills, and you'd have no cash left to deposit into your retirement and savings accounts. The latter is a critical step in rebuilding your financial health and security. You would be living paycheck to paycheck in the worst way possible."

"Is it as bleak as that?" Susan's resolve was crushed.

"You are walking through the fires of hell. Every day I speak with people who through no fault of their own are thrown into the fire, forsaken, and left to burn for others' mistakes and greed. It's not fair. I've faced demons and had my own faith tested. My family lost everything after Hurricane Katrina. They were forced to start fresh here in Seattle. I know how painful it is to have everything you care about stripped from you."

"I'm so sorry." Tina's words brought perspective.

"There were days I'd curse the sky. It was through the grace of God that I survived the wake of catastrophe. It's not easy. Healing and coming to terms with trauma and loss is an ever-evolving process. You are a work in progress. Some voids cannot be filled. You can't change the past, but you can move forward."

"It's hard to move on when everything about the life you knew was a lie. I look at my reflection now and all I see is a cracked mirror."

"You don't have to reconcile every detail. Hold close to the happy memories with Bradley, and the love you shared. Paradoxically, don't give him a pass. He betrayed you and made you suffer. You are the victim. Don't beat yourself up."

"I'm the one who was dumb enough to believe our marriage was fiscally and emotionally solvent. I should have seen through the shoddy façade. Our foundation was cracked and now I'm buried in sand. I might dig out of this financially, but emotionally…I don't know if I'll recover. Life is all about going through the motions now. I'm struggling to trust myself.

"Healing is a storm, a hurricane of the mind and soul. You can't heal by throwing your pain under the rug, allowing it to fester silently. It will grow like a cancer, until you're in a terminal state of anger. Don't allow this hurt to prevent you from moving forward. You lost your husband. He is dead and buried, but his love and betrayal leave their marks in distant stars and agonizing scars. You deserve a long cry—unleash the floodgates. Just remember that too many tears flood a soul. Allow your weeping to cleanse your heart. In mourning you walk in darkness, but remember that you still walk. Life is left to live. Release your anger, wail to the mountains, the skyscrapers, pound the sidewalks, but don't carry anger with you. The life inside of you deserves to move forward. Your future is going to be markedly different than the past, but that isn't necessarily a bad thing. God knows where you need to go. Trust his spirit. Be refined by this trial by fire," Tina encouraged.

"I don't doubt God's love but I'm struggling to move forward as my world is crumbling around me."

"When you are going through hell, keep on walking," Tina said firmly. "God himself walks with you in the fire."

"I am grateful for the cabin. I know I can overcome this trial by fire, but I'm scared to venture into this great unknown."

"Fear is the most honest expression of human nature. You are right to be scared, just don't let that fear control you. Take action. Hard as it is to hear, given the circumstances, you will be much better off if you opt for a fire sale."

"Fire sale?"

"Sell your house, sell your furniture, and get out of the impossible situation you inherited. You have a second chance. You can live rent-free in the cabin you own outright at Hidden Creek. Immerse yourself in the solitude of the lake. Perhaps this isn't a permanent solution, but it will be an anchor as you navigate the rough waters ahead. This storm will subside." Tina's savvy advice comforted Susan. As much as losing her house wounded her, she needed to start fresh.

Leaving the bank, Susan paused a moment, letting her eyes drift towards the Puget Sound. She pulled out her phone and called her friend Lisa Coley, who worked as a listing agent.

A single mother to three teenagers, Lisa empathized with the personal chaos that Susan was going through. Her husband had cheated on her, demanded a divorce, and in the process sent Lisa and her youngest daughter to the hospital trauma center. She'd regained her independence by selling real estate.

Lisa consistently ranked as one of Seattle's top Realtors. In addition to her firm, Bay Bridge Realty, Lisa owned a staging company that had been featured on HGTV.

"I know that you would rather go to the dentist than sell this house, which, given your fear of needles and drills, means this will be a horrible experience," Lisa said, trying to lighten the mood. "It isn't fair that you have to give up this dream. This house is more than brick and mortar—it has your blood, sweat, and tears in it. The hardwood floors are imprinted and worn from your footsteps. The walls echo your memories, but they also close you in. You had a good run with this house. Remember what you had here, not what you're losing.

"Impossible as it sounds, for your own sanity you must emotionally detach yourself from this process. It's just a business transaction."

"I wish it were that easy. I love this house." Susan paused. "Then I think about Bradley refinancing it for his failing business... It makes me cringe. How could he be so selfish? His actions certainly prove that the only person he cared for was himself."

"Curse Bradley if it makes you feel better. In the end, wallowing in self-pity won't provide a lasting solution," Lisa advised. "I was tempted to conjure a few voodoo hexes on my ex-husband during our divorce proceedings. In the end, a tub of ice cream and knowing my kids were safe in my arms was the only magic I needed. I know things are going to be difficult. That is an understatement. In fact, life is going to be a symphony of disaster, misery, and conflict, but through each movement you'll shed another layer of that anger, until you are free from the burden of despair. Healing will come. The time at Solitude Lake will do you a world of good."

"I'm not so sure," Susan admitted. "The lake has always been my retreat from the noise of the outside world, but it also has dark roots in my history with Bradley."

"You have to dig up dirt to bury the past."

With Lisa's keen realty sense, the Queen Anne sold within weeks of being listed. The final price was just enough to cover the mortgage plus $1,000 kickback to assist with the moving costs.

Susan sold her furniture except for a few family antiques she could squeeze into the cabin.

She traded in her luxury sedan for a used Subaru Outback. It would take four-wheel drive to maneuver the unpredictable Montana backcountry. Then she put in her two weeks' notice, saying goodbye to the life she had.

With her car packed, the widow embarked on a journey into the great unknown. Driving east on I-90 towards Missoula, her thoughts lingered on the unknown.

Returning to Hidden Creek and living at the Lone Moose had the façade of familiarity and comfort, but was frighteningly new and unresolved. The situation was a renewal of the past, a renovation of the present, and a process of being in-repair, all while instituting something that was entirely new. Uncharted territory.

The rush of racing down the interstate over mountain passes, prairies, and vast farmland was a paradox. The contradiction of a broken and unbridled spirit of release. The anticipation of her new life was ever shifting. At times Susan felt that she was climbing insurmountable mountains, only to be renewed with the energy of embracing the beauty and solidarity of the wilderness. She would then be swept up in the prairie's golden fields, only to feel crushed by the weight of heartache. Then lost in the desert, the process started over again.

Susan spent the night with her mother in Missoula to break up the nine-hour drive. Her mother had been a rock of support in this process.

"There are more than a few choice words I could pick apart when describing Bradley Dixon. He was like his father in the end, a cruel, heartless, savage jerk!"

"I don't want to talk about this right now," Susan pleaded. Her mother was verbalizing Susan's own inner thoughts. A part of her wanted to believe that there was more to the story...that her husband hadn't meant to hurt her... However, the more she learned about Bradley's deception the harder it was to trust that anything in their marriage had been real.

"Are you sure that you don't want to stay in Missoula a few more days? The Church is having a potluck and the University Club is hosting a Spring Fling event in Caras Park."

"No." Susan couldn't face socializing. No doubt the gossip chain in Missoula had been talking about her "plight" with Bradley. "The quicker I can get settled into the cabin the better."

Susan stocked up on a handful of supplies and then headed east on Highway 102 through rolling ranchland, before merging north onto MT 83. The topography quickly altered into a lush region dotted with snow and abounding lakes. Thick forests of evergreens and deciduous plant life skirted the highway, while lake after lake appeared in spectacular fashion with every bend and break in the roadside scenery.

Solitude Lake lay one mile south of Hidden Creek, off an old gravel road. A faded wooden National Forest Service sign flagged passersby to the secret wonder of the lake, otherwise obscured from the highway under the veil of a pine forest.

Solitude Lake
NFS Campgrounds: 3 miles
Solitude Lake Lodge: 5 miles

Susan paced her breaths as she turned onto Lake Drive, her heart pounding wildly. Less than a quarter mile along the rugged road, Susan veered, slamming the car brakes. Out of the forest emerged a black bear sow and her two cubs. They crossed the road with a fearless trepidation. The bear family emerging from hibernation, starving and in desperate need of food.

Susan's tear ducts filled, her emotions overwhelmed with a strange and uneasy peace.

The bears darted into the woods, cloaked in the tenuous safety of the obscurity of the forest. Susan was always shocked to see such large animals run at speeds of twenty-plus miles per hour. The bears were afraid, hungry, facing the stark reality of a wild, dangerous life. Despite the obstacles, the bears pressed on. The mother determined to provide for her cubs. The battle of life in the Rockies reinvigorated Susan. She, like her father, was captivated by nature and the lessons it taught.

With the road clear, she resumed driving, her Subaru bumping along the rough road. As the road turned a corner, the magnificence of Solitude Lake revealed itself in spectacular fashion. The icy water shimmered in the sun as a golden beacon, under the alpenglow of the towering Swan Mountains. This far corner of the mountains has always held a mysterious power over her.

"Perhaps my dad was right, maybe Solitude Lake does have the power to heal." Susan could only hope.

Chapter 4

Susan tripped over the hodgepodge of boxes infesting the cabin as she navigated her way to the kitchen, desperate for a cup of coffee. She'd had enough sense to buy a pound of City Brew Coffee's Backroads Blend when she was in Missoula. She needed the caffeine to sustain her as she delved into the daunting task of sorting through moving boxes.

Rows of boxes, tightly stacked floor to ceiling, cramping the great room and dining area, hit Susan with the inevitable realization she had been far too sentimental in the moving process. She had packed everything from dish towels to paperbacks she'd never read again. The unpacking process would be a true spring cleaning. Now if only she could find the box cutter.

Susan was several hours knee deep into her decluttering effort when she heard a heavy knock on the front door. She assumed it was the property's caretaker, Noah Armistead, who had mentioned he'd stop by. As she opened the door, she was pleasantly surprised to be greeted by two of her lake neighbors, Beth and Glen Matheson.

The Mathesons lived just south of the Lone Moose, in the Meadowlark Retreat. The couple, in their upper sixties, were longtime residents of Solitude Lake. Glen was a semiretired professor at the University of Montana, where he taught

Natural Sciences. Beth was a retired librarian, who was active in the Hidden Creek community. The couple spent late April through mid-October at Solitude Lake. The rest of the year they split between Missoula and two months in Arizona to be close to their family (not to mention a break from the endless Montana winter).

"Sorry to barge in, but we heard through the grapevine that you arrived in town and wanted to ensure that you were well fed." Glen kicked the snow off his boots before stepping inside.

"We thought you could use a pick-me-up in this cold, wet weather." Beth presented Susan with a welcome basket. "Fresh-out-of-the-oven huckleberry muffins drizzled in my signature sweet cream sauce, hot chocolate mix, and a handful of other goodies to whet your appetite."

"This is a wonderful surprise. Please come in. I will warn you—the cabin is a war zone. The movers dropped off my things yesterday. I'm afraid I wasn't as frugal in the keep-it-or-junk-it round of packing."

"I hear that you'll be a year-round resident of Solitude Lake." Beth shifted the subject.

"That is the plan, at least for now."

"I ran into Marjorie Hatfield at the Timber's Edge last week. She mentioned that you accepted a teaching position at Hidden Creek High School?"

"I'll be teaching English, as well as American History starting in the fall. I'll admit, the position will be a challenge after spending the past ten years working with third graders. I'm thrilled to have the opportunity dig into Chaucer, Shakespeare to Thoreau and Hawthorne, Hardy, Austen, Dickens. I have an excuse to be a lit nerd again."

For a second, Susan thought about the antique copy of *Great Expectations*. She refused to sell it, perhaps a silly move given the potential value In fact, the book was the first thing that she had unpacked, placing it in her grandfather's study in a temperature-controlled safe.

"It is good to have you home." Beth said warmly. "You made a wise decision. Solitude Lake has the power to heal even the most broken in spirit."

"We were sorry to learn about Bradley's death." Glen broached the topic. An awkward pause ensued.

"It has been a difficult time. Thank you for sending the flowers and note in the wake of my husband's death."

Susan wondered how much detail the Mathesons knew about the aftermath of Bradley's death. Beth and Beatrix were great friends. No doubt Beatrix Blanchard had clued them in on her daughter's backstage drama. It wasn't that Beatrix was a gossip—far from it. She knew that her daughter needed a strong support system, and the people of Hidden Creek would be willing to step up to the challenge, without judging Susan.

For the next hour, the neighbors caught up while indulging in scrumptious huckleberry muffins and a steaming pot of Earl Grey tea.

"We would be happy to stay and help you rifle through these boxes," Glen offered.

"Thanks for the offer, but I need to sort through this muck alone."

"Let's meet up for lunch later week," Beth suggested. "Everyone wants to welcome you home. We can reserve the back room at the Timber's Edge Café to celebrate."

"I don't want you to go to any trouble."

"No trouble at all. I'll contact you with the details. In the interim, don't hesitate to give us a ring if you need anything."

"A quick reminder that the loons are nesting," Glen advised. "We don't have any nests on this edge of the lake, but there are quite a few breeding spots. If the mother loon gets startled from human activity, they will abandon their young."

"I'll be careful."

Glen was always a go-to for the latest flora and fauna report. He volunteered at the Hidden Creek Ranger Station, oversaw the local Birding Society, and gave weekly fireside naturalist chats during the peak summer season at Solitude

Lake. Glen reminded Susan of her father. The two had been close friends.

Susan continued to fumble through the boxes. She knew that this process would take several weeks. Each box *was* stuffed with memories and emotional gravity. She didn't want to delay the cleaning process, but she didn't want to rush it either. She needed to let go of the loose ends in her own time, piece by piece, and in this case, box by box.

Noah Armistead stopped by the Lone Moose just after four o'clock. At fifty-six years of age, with a thick head of gray hair and blue eyes, Noah had served as a trusted employee and friend of the Blanchard family for over forty years. He had started off as a summer employee at Blanchard's Pharmacy, now known as Swan Valley Pharmacy. After going to technical school to become an electrician and plumber, Noah found a niche servicing as a winter caretaker for lake homes. He ensured that the property was winterized and kept in top turnkey condition for his clients. To Susan he was an uncle of sorts, the kind that you could rely on to get you out of a bind, especially when your toilet overflowed at two in the morning and the heat went out during a snowstorm.

"Pretty as always. You look like your mother but have your daddy's green eyes."

"Can I interest you in one of Beth Matheson's famed glazed huckleberry muffins?"

"No thanks. Annie wants me to watch my weight before we go to our niece's wedding in Chouteau to fit into the new suit she bought me." The handyman hesitated. "Aw, what the hell, I've been restricted to salads and protein shakes the past three weeks. A muffin will do me a world of good."

"I appreciate your work to keep this place standing."

"The Lone Moose has a special place in my heart." Noah paused. "I will admit that I was shocked when I learned that you planned to live in the cabin year-round. You'll be one of only five year-round residents on the lake in the winter. Don't get me wrong. I'll have this place in tip-top shape for winter living…it is just so isolated here."

"I could use some solitude in my life."

Susan knew that Noah had never cared for Bradley. Though he'd never been outright rude to her husband, Noah made it clear that he worked for Susan Blanchard and not Bradley Daly Dixon.

When Noah learned of Susan's engagement, he had been quick to point out Brad's shortcomings and his reasons for advising against the marriage. Once she had made her decision, Noah reprimanded her once, speaking his piece and then shutting up. He regretted that Susan had to live with such harsh consequences from Bradley's mistakes.

"I'm sorry about what that heartless jerk did to you. Remember that Annie and I are here for you."

"I appreciate that." Susan mustered a smile. "I have a list of odd jobs I need help with to get everything ready for summer."

"I'm already on it," Noah affirmed. "Next week I'll have the kayaks out and the boat house de-winterized...that is if winter is kind enough to leave."

After touching base with Noah, Susan decided to head into town. Her fridge was bare except for a carton of half and half. Grocery shopping was long overdue. Plus, it would be nice to leave the mess of the cabin for several hours.

Susan tumbled over the gravel road, driving past the Eagle Point National Forest Campground, before hitting 83.

The jumbled sky, a contradiction in motion, was half blue and cloudless, and half dark gray with heavy rain and intermittent snow. Susan's heart skipped a beat as she entered the city limits of Hidden Creek.

Welcome to Hidden Creek: Land of Lakes, Forests and Mountains...The sign was placed meticulously in front of the visitor center.

Hidden Creek was anchored by its historic downtown, which paralleled MT 83. The four-block city center boasted a variety of businesses, from eateries to art galleries, banks, general stores and suppliers, a bowling alley...all the essentials. Eateries such as the Coyote Grill, Glacier Coffee Company and Flathead Bakery, the Timber's Edge Café, Big Dipper Drive-In, and the five-star Swan Bistro gave locals and tourists a mix of culinary options. Glacier Bank and First West Bank were stationed across from the post office, Hidden Creek Ranger Station, and City Hall. In addition to area camping and lake lodges, Hidden Creek was home to the Elkhorn Motor Lodge and the Sunrise Bed & Breakfast. Other businesses filling out the retail corridor: Swan Valley Pharmacy, True Value and Ace Hardware, Hidden Fly Shop, Mystic Outfitters, and Emmett's Mercantile and General Store. The library lay two blocks east on Seeley Road, across from the Community Building, which housed a senior center, gymnasium, and theater. Neighborhoods of early-nineteenth-century to mid-sixties architecture filled out the east and west corridor of town. The Blanchard family had lived in the apartment above the pharmacy. The current owner of the buildings had turned the space into offices.

The Swan Valley Grocery Store was locally owned and rivaled any national competitor. The grocer stocked its shelves with the best in organic specialty foods and national brands. The butcher, Randy Kessler, ran the premier meat department in Montana, with farm-raised chicken, grass-fed beef, local game, and fine deli meats. The staff at Swan Valley Grocery knew each of their customers by name.

Susan found herself in the ice-cream aisle. A dangerous spot. She didn't have much of a sweet tooth, but ice cream always did her in. She picked up a gallon of Wilcoxson's Stuck in a Rut, setting it down in her cart.

She slashed through a two-page shopping list that included everything from milk to vegetables, cereal and crackers, condiments, wine and chocolate, meat, cheeses…anything and everything for a week's worth of meals that would fit in her fridge and freezer.

Susan was in the juice aisle when she crashed into an unsuspecting customer.

"I'm so sorry. I was distracted," she muttered.

"If it isn't Susan Blanchard?" an all-too-familiar voice sounded.

"Jake…" She strained to compose herself. Jake Arnett had been her best friend since they were three. His family owned the Solitude Lake Lodge on the far side of the lake—it was there that they'd spent six wonderful summers as staff members of the lodge dining room. It had been three years since she'd last run into Jake. It was a welcome yet awkward surprise given their history.

There was a brief silence. Jake stood just over six foot four, with tussled brown hair, hazel eyes, a chiseled jaw, and dimples. He looked Susan over. It was hard. They shared a long history and a past that he had never truly gotten over.

"It isn't like a Blanchard to go speechless." Jake never mentioned the last name Dixon. The pain still cut too deeply. He could never reconcile the fact that she had married Bradley Daly Dixon.

"It is great to see you." Susan spoke the truth. She hated that they had grown apart. Jake had always been her anchor. He would always bear the distinction of "best friend," even if they had barely spoken in the past fifteen years.

"You look radiant." Jake had missed Susan. She haunted his thoughts daily. To Susan, Jake was a friend, but to him…she was the world. Jake had loved Susan since they were kids. Perhaps he was bitter that she chose Brad over him. Seeing Susan again was a whirlwind. It unearthed suppressed feelings he wasn't quite sure how to handle.

"You're not looking too bad yourself." Susan bit her lip. He looked as handsome as ever. "I appreciate the package you sent back in January. It meant a lot to me." Jake had mailed a condolence letter to Susan with a box of pictures of Bradley, Jake, and Susan from their days working together.

"I know that Bradley's death was hard on you…" Jake empathized. Through the grapevine he'd been able to piece together the estate mess. Anger at the deceased burned like a fire within him. He hurt for Susan's loss, but cursed Bradley.

"I sold my house in Seattle. I've moved into the Lone Moose on a permanent basis."

"That is news." Jake had heard Susan might be coming back to town for a few weeks, but to learn she was in the area for good—it was almost too much to bear.

"I'm going to work at the high school in the fall. In the interim I'm looking for summer work to keep me busy. That is, after I finish unpacking the horde I lugged with me from Seattle."

"I'd love to catch up over dinner." The words slipped out. Jake wanted to share a meal with Susan, but a part of him knew that reconnecting with her could lead them both down a dangerous path. He had barely survived the first broken heart; he wouldn't survive another.

"That would be fun..." Susan couldn't refuse, but also wondered if dinner was the best idea. "Why don't you come to Café Lone Moose? I have a new recipe I'd like to try out and as you can see from my shopping cart, my kitchen will be stocked."

"Give me the time and date and I'll be there," Jake replied without hesitation.

"Wednesday, eight o'clock?"

"Perfect."

Chapter 5

Fire red burst through the lingering clouds, a warm glow as daylight shifted into dusk. Solitude Lake, ever still, flickered with vibrant color as the water lapped. The ice had broken significantly in the past week. Summer's kiss thawing the land.

Jake drove his truck into a roadside ditch. Standing between the pines, he surveyed the horizon, the fresh scent of the forest filling his lungs. For a moment time stood still, the past and future fused as one. Summer soon would melt the frozen heart of winter.

As Jake touched the water, he shivered. Solitude Lake was still too frigid for swimming, but within a month beachgoers would pack the lake's sandy shores, basking in the effervescent sun with water. Swimmers and kayakers enjoying the water with effortless ease.

"Only a few weeks before the Solitude Lake Lodge is open for business, celebrating its eighty-fifth anniversary." Jake pondered his own history, growing up at the lake and his past with Susan.

Jake looked south towards the Lone Moose. The cabin was built on Osprey Point, a peninsula that jutted out into the lake. Susan's scent, lilac, still fresh on his senses from their encounter.

He mulled over her return to the lake. It carried an emotional toll. He battled feelings of joy, regret, and fear. Above all he felt solace. Solace in knowing that the woman he loved was so desperately close, even if her heart was unattainable.

After getting back in his truck, Jake drove lakeside for several miles before turning into the service entrance of the Solitude Lake Lodge.

Nestled amid a dense forest, this off-the-beaten-path resort straddled pristine shores of crystal blue waters. The resort offered mountain charm, fine dining, authentic Montana hospitality, spectacular scenery, and infinite recreation opportunities.

The lodge's history dated to 1924, when Isaak Belton (Emmett's son) purchased ten miles of shoreline and twenty areas of neighboring wilderness. His purpose was to build a guest ranch that would fit the needs of a variety of travelers.

Ned Blanchard provided Isaak Belton with the architectural blueprint for the lodge. Blanchard and Belton's vision was to design a retreat to showcase the scenic treasure and rustic charm of the region, while remaining refined enough to lure in *worldly* travelers.

The architecture was engineered to humbly reflect the imagery and majesty of the land. Most of the construction was derived from local raw materials. The interior design was inspired by Montana culture with a taste of Alpine couture. C.M. Russell, a patron of the lodge, was commissioned by Belton to paint several pieces of Western artwork, including the Solitude Wrangler Murals. Russell's epic canvas remained in the lodge's grand entryway and Whistling Elk Saloon as a toast to the wild untamed restless solitude of the land.

The main lodge dated to 1924 and was the oldest building on-site; except for Isaak Belton's one-bedroom cabin, which currently served as the Crafts Nook. The main lodge included fifteen guest rooms, a grand lobby, ballroom, and library as well as the Whistling Elk Saloon and Solitude Dining Room.

Seventeen additional cabins, dating from 1933 to 1978, scattered the property. The cabins ranged in size from one to three bedrooms. The lodge also boasted a recreational barn, boat house and docks, arts and crafts cabin, gift shop featuring Montana-made and local-artisan crafts, a stable, and staff dorms. The lodge staffed thirty-five full-time and half a dozen part-time workers in the summer months.

The Arnett family had owned the Solitude Lake Lodge for seventy years. The soil and foundation was in Jake's family's DNA. It was their heritage and lifeblood. Jake's mother referred to it as "sweet desolation." Seven to eight months out of the year, the lake was frozen, locked by winter; the inhabitants of the lodge were dependent on cross-country skis, snow mobiles, chained trucks, and modern technologies such as broadband internet and phone service to connect to the outside world. It was a desolate and cold, yet strikingly beautiful existence.

While some souls hungered for the frigid frost of winter, wandering restlessly in the cold smoke on skis on virgin snow; Jake saw winter as a means to an end. He puts up with winter because it breathed life into summer. Summer at Solitude Lake was the closest part of heaven's stratosphere on earth. The season was a time of magic and ceaseless beauty. Winter is a long drought in a dying breath before the eloquence of summer's conversation. With Susan back at the lake, the fire of summer's flame burned all the brighter for Jake.

"I'm home," Jake called out as he entered the four-bedroom cabin he shared with his parents, Molly and Walter Arnett.

At thirty-eight, Jake was the only child still living on the property. His sister, Keeley, lived with her husband in Hidden Creek proper. Keeley serves as the operations manager with her brother, Jake, for the main lodge. Jake's older brothers, Gilligan and Russ, managed the Whistling Elk Saloon and

Solitude Dining Room, respectively. The lodge was a family-run business, each member pulling their weight.

"It took you long enough to get home. I was beginning to think you had gotten mauled by a grizzly," Molly teased her son. Molly Arnett was sixty-five years young, with slightly graying auburn curls and vibrant green eyes. She lived up to her reputation of being a no-nonsense spitfire.

"I ran into Susan Blanchard at the grocery store." Jake's words cut the air like a rusted train racing off a bridge.

"Oh?" Molly's motherly instinct was on guard as she pressed her lips together apprehensively.

There was a time when Molly prayed that she might have the chance to call Susan her daughter-in-law. That was before Susan eloped with Bradley Dixon...breaking her son Jake's heart. The fault was not entirely Susan's. Jake allowed fear to hide his true feelings for Susan until it was too late. Molly feared Susan's return could rupture sealed scars; her presence was salt in the wound for Jake.

"She's moved back into the Lone Moose permanently..." Jake recognized his mother's ambivalence. "She has a job lined up at the high school, starting in the fall."

"That is news." Molly raised her right brow to feign surprise. Beatrix Blanchard had phoned Molly weeks ago to clue her into Susan's plight as a widow and her return to the lake.

"Susan was kind enough to invite me to dinner at her place on Wednesday. I accepted."

"Is that a good idea?" Molly's frown was accusatory.

"We've been best friends since we were toddlers. Why wouldn't it be a good idea?" Jake shrugged.

"It's your history that scares me."

"She needs a friend right now."

"Susan has plenty of friends in town to console her. I don't want you tangled up in her web."

"Web? Susan isn't a black widow, ready to bite me with toxic venom." Jake was infuriated by his mother's reaction. "You know darn well that she is a strong and caring person.

She doesn't deserve animosity, but compassion in the wake of what that husband put her through."

"You misjudge my respect for Susan *Dixon*. I think the world of her. What I don't want is for you to latch on to her. She is vulnerable right now. If your relationship goes further than friendship, you'll wind up with another broken heart. I don't think the shattered pieces will be put back together this time."

"In terms of love, I got over Susan a long time ago. What I don't want to lose is our friendship."

Molly sighed. She resigned herself to the fact that her son was stubborn as he was blind in love. It was a lesson he would have to learn the hard way.

Chapter 6

"Bradley, you are a lying piece of crud!" Susan screamed, bursting into tears as she hurled their wedding portrait at the cabin's stone fireplace.

It had been a draining day. The seemingly mundane task of sifting through boxes had erupted into a renewed discord. She knew it was part of the healing process to peel back the emotional layers, allowing herself to come to terms with each stratum bit by excruciating bit. But psychological awareness didn't make the process any easier.

Bradley left secrets lurking in the shadows. The secrets tormented her with questions and riddles. It was an enigma she would probably never solve. Bradley was dead, answers buried six feet under. Still one question incessantly beat on her brain: Why?

As Susan fumbled through the horde of boxes, a small ray of hope emerged.

"Bible Verses for the Broken-Hearted." Susan picked up the paperback. Shifting through the devotional, she was drawn to a passage from Philippians, 4:6–7.

"Be careful for nothing; but in everything by prayer and supplication with thanksgiving let your requests be made known unto God. And the peace of God, which passeth all understanding, shall keep your hearts and minds through Christ Jesus."

Since Bradley's death, worry spread like a virus in Susan. Anxiety constantly controlled her thoughts. Her mind replaying flashbacks of a life, she saw a constant loop of failures and disaster. Nights were the worst. The silence of sleep filled with nightmares and panic attacks. Her innate nature clung to the habit of holding everything in and trying to compartmentalize her stress. It was hard for her to let go of control. Perhaps that was why she clung to the worry so fiercely. Anxiety became a shield of sorts—a toxic sword of protection.

Her faith, though tested, remained strong in the bereavement process. Susan knew that she needed to relinquish the fear, such a toxic power, and turn her worry over to God. She knew that God heard her supplications, whether they be curses or petitions. She needed the Holy Spirit to guide her through this process, instead of leaning into the revenge and hate that often tempted her. This faith didn't mean that God would suddenly part the clouds and clear her path, but it was a light in the darkness, or better yet a lighthouse in the fog. It might be a bumpy road, but if she held firm to that hope, she would emerge from this, not necessarily better off financially, but spiritually whole.

Per Lisa's advice, Susan had spoken with a therapist and a bereavement counselor, and a parish priest in Seattle.

The process, though helpful, was disjointed. At the time, Susan had been too overwhelmed with the brunt of her husband's death and betrayal to uncork her emotions. She did not want to reveal her secrets, instead pretending as if things were normal. She quit therapy, further isolating her pain and anxiety from the outside world. Her life had morphed into a lonely island—a house atop a rock, with a foundation built on sand. She ran feverishly searching for a place to hide.

Bradley had been active in their parish in Seattle, volunteering at the soup kitchen, helming the youth group ski trip, giving his time for Operation Construction to End

Homelessness... He had done a lot of good in the world. Susan liked to think that the benevolent side of Bradley reflected his core, and the corroded parts were just a cruel façade—a front by a boy still confused and angry from years of his father's abuse...

The verse from Philippians served as a reminder. Self-reliance and contemplation were important components in the healing process—true healing came from God alone. It would take the power of the Holy Trinity, as well as friends and family, to lead her out of this foreign, lonely land.

Susan made her way to the cabin's kitchen. She hesitated before picking up the vintage rotary phone. Bradley had installed the phone four years ago during a minor kitchen remodel. He insisted that after eighty-six years' devoid of phone service, the Lone Moose needed to be brought into the twenty-first century.

Dialing Saint Michael's Church, Susan made an appointment to meet with parish priest Father Leo. Father Leo had been her priest from age ten up. He had presided over her wedding and knew Bradley's flaws and triumphs. Most importantly, she felt comfortable confiding in him.

"Ice cream isn't the healthiest way to mend a broken heart, but it sure tastes delicious," Susan teased herself as she grabbed the carton of Stuck in a Rut from the freezer. She savored each bite of the chocolate, creamy caramel blended in home-churned vanilla ice cream.

She spent the rest of the evening going through boxes, tangled up in memories she had to throw in the dumpster. Starting fresh was hard, but necessary.

Chapter 7

Morning broke as the mountain sun flooded the Lone Moose. Rubbing her sleepy eyes, Susan glanced at the bedside clock. 7 a.m. She pulled the covers over her head, desperate to fall back into dreams, but the intense glare of the sun refused to be ignored.

Begrudgingly she rose from the comfort and security of the bed. Too lazy to change out of her weathered knit L.L. Bean pajamas, she put on her slippers and staggered to the kitchen to brew a pot of coffee.

"It is going to be a pretty day," Susan said, trying to be upbeat as she looked out the window. She had a busy schedule: lunch with Beth and some friends at the Timber's Edge at one o'clock, and an appointment with Father Leo at four.

This morning, though, Susan's primary task was to find a summer job. She had enough in savings to tide her over, but she needed to ensure she had cash coming in. Plus, a job would keep her occupied, get her mind away from pity parties and moping.

Finding seasonal work scared her. It had been fifteen years since she last waited tables, manned cash registers, served as a clerical aide and navigated the chaos of retail... She was up for the task but feared that she'd be behind the times compared to tech savvy high school and college students. In truth, she desired quiet days by the lake with a book, not the hectic hustle and bustle of a gift shop or diner.

Downing two successive cups of black coffee, Susan cut through the hallway, past the laundry room to the study. Sitting down in her grandfather's knotted pine office chair, her gaze wandered to the list of cabin rules she'd love as a child.

Lone Moose Cabin Rules:
1. Relax
2. Fish, tip a canoe, swim, repeat
3. Sit on the dock, feet in the water, basking in the sun
4. Hike, climb mountains, cross streams
5. Don't feed the bears
6. Rise with the sun, fall asleep with the moon
7. Trace the stars
8. Ignite campfires, eat s'mores
9. Get Lost in the woods to be found
10. Discover Solitude

Her focus rested on rule number ten: *Discover Solitude*. Ned Blanchard had nailed the rules in the study as a reminder that the cabin wasn't a second office. She would have to make an exception, just this once.

She powered on her laptop. After tweaking her résumé, Susan printed off twenty copies, along with reference letters, then she grabbed the paper to look at the classifieds.

Hidden Creek had one newspaper, the *Lake Gazette*. The periodical hit newsstands on Thursdays and detailed the local roundup of news. Most businesses relied on storefront want ads when recruiting seasonal employees, so the classifieds section was slim, but Susan didn't let that get her down.

She showered and pulled together a cute outfit—jeans with a hand-knit cardigan and snow boots.

The fact that Hidden Creek was a small town was a blessing and a curse. Everyone within fifty miles knew that Susan Dixonwas reeling from the loss of her husband. Thanks to Beatrix Blanchard, the whole town was probably aware that Bradley Dixon had disinherited his wife and burned through his inheritance and fortune, leaving poor broken Susan in a terrible mess.

The Hidden Creek community had always had an ambivalent view of Bradley Daly Dixon. His reputation spanned from all-star athlete, drop-dead-gorgeous charmer, honorable Boy Scout, and hard worker, to guilty by association through the DNA of his corrupt father. Since his death the general opinion around town had turned to disdain. Susan was dearly loved and Bradley's betrayal of her was deemed a betrayal of the town itself.

Susan vacillated in her opinions of her deceased husband, searching for threads of evidence to prove his betrayal wasn't rooted in malice. Perhaps his father's shadow had haunted Bradley so long that the darkness had caved in on him. Those were questions she wouldn't have answers to in this lifetime.

Susan thought about Bradley's parents. His mother, Elana, had died two years ago. Her death was strange and sudden, as Elana collapsed over the railing of her Victorian-era home in Butte. She'd remarried a man named Jeff Sayers shortly after Bradley graduated from the University of Washington. Jeff, a geologist, had been doing fieldwork, studying geyser and earthquake activity in Yellowstone National Park when the accident occurred. Like Bradley, he believed that Elana had been murdered. The Butte authorities pined over the case for a year before concluding that it was accidental. The cause: Mrs. Elana Sayers had a stroke, and in the process, she slipped and fell over the railing.

Bradley never bought the police's explanation. Obsessed with finding out the truth, he became convinced that his father, washed up in his political career, had killed his mother as an act of revenge. He confronted his father on the issue, which resulted in a bar fight in Helena. Behavior atypical for Bradley, who never touched alcohol. His father, who was in Austin, Texas, at the time of Elana's death, was absolved of any wrongdoing. Bradley and his father never spoke again. Ellis Dixon hadn't even bothered to come to Bradley's funeral.

No doubt the difficult relationship with his father tainted Bradley. Susan had tried to reconcile his mother's tragic death and final blow with his father as a trigger for his erratic spending and gambling. Unfortunately, records proved that this behavior had gone on years before her death.

Susan kicked off her job search at Marmot Books and Coffee. The funky shop was housed inside a three-bedroom bungalow in the heart of downtown. The award-winning independent bookstore was a favorite haunt in Hidden Creek. The store specialized in regional literature and nonfiction as well as stocking thousands of titles in every subject and genre, be it the obscure academic textbook or fast-selling gripping crime drama.

The store was owned by local Lacy Riggs and Portland transplant Nick Crosby. The coffee shop and eatery offered readers the perfect nook to relax with a paperback while warming up with a latte and teacake. Wine and beer from Flathead area breweries were on the menu every afternoon for Wine & Read Happy Hour.

A bibliophile, Susan loved the atmosphere of bookstores. The process of picking a random book off the shelf and letting it sweep her into an adventure tantalized her senses. Now more than ever, she yearned to skim the paragraphs of a strange novel, letting her mind dance into a world of plots as characters escaped the pages.

The Marmot was Susan's ideal job, a place to share her passion for the written word while conversing with locals and tourists.

Susan and Lacy were longtime friends. Susan knew if a position was available, it would be offered.

"If it isn't Blancher!" Lacy, five foot four and petite with a short bob and funky glasses, referred to Susan's childhood nickname. "The word on the street is that you're our newest permanent resident."

"News spreads fast here." Susan managed a smile. "The shop looks amazing."

"The hours of DIY binge-watching paid off. Nick and I spruced the place up."

"You always have the shop in tip-top condition," Susan held. "I saw that you were featured in *Sunset Magazine* as a top five best indie bookseller in the Northwest."

"Thank you! It is an honor. Are you here to stock up on summer reading?" Lacy's eyes lit up at the mere mention of books. "A new thriller set in Glacier National Park was just released. Nonstop action set against the natural drama of the park. You'd adore it. I also recommend the new page-turner *Big Sky Country*, a romance novel without the sentimental ruckus." Lacy knew that Susan didn't like sentimental books. For a romance novel to be deemed acceptable it required depth, conflict, and raw hard-hitting reality.

"I'm actually here to apply for a job." Susan mustered the courage to broach the topic, presenting her résumé and references.

Lacy knew that things hadn't been easy for Susan, but she was a little surprised Susan was in the market for a summer job.

"A job?"

"My retail credentials are dated, though you will find my expertise in literature far-reaching from popular fiction to classics and nonfiction. I come with a strong work ethic and positive attitude. I'm willing to commit to either full-time or a part-time seasonal position"

"Isn't it best to take the summer off? You deserve a chance to relax and recuperate before jumping into your new position at the high school."

"I wish it were that simple. The fact is that I need the money."

Lacy's face fell, hearing the exasperation in her friend's voice. She didn't press for details. It was obvious that Bradley's estate had provided so little to sustain his widow that she didn't have the luxury of a summer break, even though she had a salaried job commencing in the fall.

"I wish that you had applied a few weeks back. I hired five seasonal full-time workers in April, who are already in training. I could squeeze schedules and try to fit you in somewhere, but I'm afraid there wouldn't be much money involved."

"Early bird gets the worm." Susan pulled her composure. "If anything changes, let me know."

"While you're in the shop, let's catch up over coffee, my treat."

Susan left the Marmot forty minutes later, her stomach content after a delectable slice of apple crumb cake and a Glacier Chai Latte. Lacy insisted on sending her off with a tote bag full of used and new books for summer reading.

Disappointed, albeit determined, Susan pressed on. Over the next two hours, she hit the pavement, dropping off résumés at various downtown shops, offices, and restaurants. Though there was plenty of interest, she failed to lasso any firm job offers.

By one o'clock, the sustenance of the coffee and crumb cake had worn thin. She paced down Front Street to meet her friends for lunch.

The Timber's Edge Café was midway down Front Street.

To passersby, the Timber's Edge appeared to be a leftover icon from a bygone era, with a retro 1960s sign that could use a paint touch-up. Inside, the diner's warm throwback Montana atmosphere was alive with energy. The restored soda fountain was filled with locals sharing the latest news over coffee or a Flathead Lake Huckleberry Soda. Tables and booths were crammed into the rest of the space like a rotary club function. Historic town photos were hung on the walls, alongside antique Great Northern Railway posters. The posters were designed to market Northwestern Montana's romantic

Western beauty. If only train travel were still so mysteriously exciting.

In terms of food, you wouldn't find a better breakfast spot in the Swans. The Timber's Edge was renowned for its succulent cinnamon rolls. The recipe was guarded heavily, jokingly referred to as Grandma Maeve's trade secret. Ranchers drove as far as fifty miles to eat the enormous Westerner Omelet and slightly smaller Cowboy Delight, accompanied by crispy thick bacon and hand-fired griddle cakes.

"You've finally wised up, left that rainy city, and found your way back home." Ever peppy, highly organized head waitress Missy Evaro welcomed her friend and patron into the restaurant. "Beth and the girls are in the Angler's Room waiting for you. Do you fancy the usual, Dancing Bear Omelet with a side of home sliced hash browns?"

"Your memory never fails." It felt good to be back in Hidden Creek. It felt good to call it home.

Beth, always the social planner, had managed to round up ten mutual friends for the informal lunch party. When Susan entered the Angler's Banquet Room, chatter erupted as the group welcomed their friend back home.

"Simmer down." Beth whistled to reel in the crowd. "Give Susan some space. You'll each have time to say your hellos and ask questions."

Sitting down at the table, Susan took notice of those that surrounded her. On the far right was Stevie Smith, the best horse trainer and wrangler in the city limits.

"Thunder heard you're back in town. You ready to get on the saddle again?" Stevie referred to Thunder, the dark mustang she'd broken two years back. Susan had a deep fear of horseback riding. She fell off a horse at age ten, breaking her leg. Still, she had shared a sort of magic on the backcountry trail with Thunder.

"He's the only horse that didn't throw me off the saddle. How are things at the Hidden Creek Guest Ranch?"

"We're gearing up for high season. June's packing trips are fully booked, and July is not far behind. I'm finalizing details on the summer rodeo runs. First Friday Rodeo and Second Sunday Rodeos, looks to be a hot ticket."

The ranch was a combination inn–horse breeding farm, with a small herd of cattle, mostly to give tourists a run for their money. It was the go-to place in town for riding lessons and horseback packing trips. They ran the best rodeos in the valley, fun for all ages.

Seated next to Stevie was Harley Ethlers, a mechanic at her father's service station. Looking at Harley, petite with a blond bob and blue eyes, dressed to a T in Ralph Lauren, you'd never guess she was the best transmission and engine fixer in town. There was a time she'd even competed at the Flathead Motorway in Kalispell.

"You're due for an oil change after that move."

"I planned to make an appointment next week." Susan had never dealt with car maintenance. That was Bradley's job. She was grateful that Harley was around to help with tire rotations, compressors, air filters, and oil changes.

Farther down the line was Marion McCloud, owner of the Bird Woman Art Gallery. The gallery showcased Montana artists, with an emphasis on Blackfoot and Flathead Native American artisans. Marion's dad, Miller, owned Yogo Jewelry next door.

"I'm planning an arts festival for mid-July—it would be great to get you on the planning committee, given your keen artistic eye."

"That sounds fun," Susan tentatively agreed. "I noticed the new hand=blown glass jewelry in your shop window—stunning."

"It's designed by a Blackfoot artisan up in Browning. Each piece tells a story."

Susan held a passion for Native American culture, artwork, and storytelling. The thought of a piece of jewelry connecting to the individual energy of a person, a living story, was provoking.

Susan played with her wedding ring. Bradley bought her the Yogo Sapphire from McCloud years ago. It was hard to part with a ring that had so much history...even if she knew financially, she should sell it.

Gretchen Kline, who was in her upper seventies, was head owner of the Elkhorn Motor Inn with her son Steve. She had a sharp sense of humor and far more energy than the rest of the table combined, hiking to Swan Peak every July.

Karen Kincaid had purchased Blanchard's Pharmacy with her husband, Phil, shortly after Susan's father died, renaming it the Swan Valley Pharmacy. It was the only full-service pharmacy for forty miles, complete with an ice-cream counter. Despite the circumstances of Karen and Phil coming to town, Susan had grown close with the couple. She appreciated the energy and dedication they'd thrown into SVP, following her dad's legacy.

"We're so happy you're back." Darcy Evans hugged Susan. Darcy was a lovable busybody who worked at Hidden Creek General Store.

"We are sorry about the circumstances, but beyond thrilled to have our hometown girl back," Nettie Graves added. Nettie was the head librarian; she'd taught Susan how to read. The woman possessed a rare voice that could make a story fly like lightning to a young reader. Nettie's budget had been significantly cut, which meant currently she was the only full-time staff librarian. The community had rallied around the Fund Our Library cause, but it was hard to convince county officers to fund a small-town outpost.

"We'll have to do some hiking once everything is thawed out," Kate Morgan suggested. She was thirty-two and worked as an interpretive ranger at the Hidden Creek Forestry Station. She also volunteered with the local Hidden Hiking Club and Loon Society.

"Jake said that you were back in town." Keeley Hensley, nee Arnett, was full of warmth and curiosity. "It's good to have you back at Solitude Lake."

Keeley meant it too. She had babysat Jake and Susan when they were five- and six-year-olds. Susan was a sister of sorts. Keeley only wished that with Bradley out of the picture, Jake and Susan could pick up where they left off sixteen years ago.

"How are the twins?" Susan referenced Keeley's seven-year-old twin boys, Max and Grayer.

"Grayer is a future angler and cowboy like his granddaddy Arnett. Max will follow my husband into the field of law, I'm afraid." Keeley's husband, Holden, was one of three attorneys in town. He dabbled in defense, estates, and ranch mergers.

The next two hours flew by as the friends caught up. There was plenty of local "news" to share from the creek. Susan mentioned her search for a summer job, which yielded some quality leads.

The elephant in the room remained Bradley Dixon. He was a despised man among Susan's friends. Montanans didn't have a smooth knack for communicating. They could be overly blunt and at times rude. When it came to matters of grieving and betrayal, it was easier just to bake someone a cake and avoid the conversation.

"Time has flown," Susan said, noticing the time. "I'm due to meet Father Leo at St. Michael's in twenty minutes."

"Don't be a stranger. We're here to help."

As Susan exited the restaurant, Keeley stopped her.

"I was forced to fire our Children's Activity Coordinator this morning for unruly and reckless behavior. The lodge desperately needs a reliable, dynamic, credentialed replacement." Keeley was blunt. "I want you to work at the lodge."

"Are you sure that I'm the ideal candidate?" Susan hesitated.

"You have a strong history with the lodge—heck, your great-grandfather designed the place. Add in your tenure as an elementary school teacher—yes, I'd say that you are more than qualified." Keeley was clearly putting her foot down. "Come to the lodge tomorrow morning, at ten o'clock. I'll fill you in on the job description and salary, and we can take care of all paperwork."

"I'll be there," Susan stammered, befuddled by what had just transpired. From the looks of it, she had a job, at her old stomping grounds. She pondered if it was the best place to kick up the dirt.

Chapter 8

Saint Michael's was on the corner of Olive and Grinnell Streets, across from the Belton City Park. The church foundation dated to 1910, when Hidden Creek was an ill-placed mining camp. Built in a gothic revival style, the sanctuary expanded in 1938, while the rectory, parish hall, offices, and classrooms dated to the mid-1960s. The diverse congregation was active in worship and outreach.

"You're late." Father Leo tsked.

"I lost track of time," Susan admitted. "Beth Matheson arranged a lunch party, an informal welcome back to Hidden Creek affair. Will a slice of chocolate moose tracks pie abate my tardiness?"

"I am ashamed that you would resort to bribing a priest with chocolate." Leo's sternness broke into a smile, revealing his ruse. "For the record, I'm notoriously tardy and could never judge you for a five-minute delay. As for the pie, I shouldn't accept. Then again, it is a sin to let a complimentary piece of pie go to waste, especially since I've been starving myself on my diet. Since St. Michael's started our ninety-day boot camp in March, I've lost fifteen pounds."

"Boot camp?"

"It's a health regimen for mind, body, and soul. It includes exercise classes in the church community center, a series of lectures on health, and a Bible study that helps to motivate and encourage us in the health improvement journey, while feeding our soul with spiritual nourishment."

St. Michael's had never played into its size. What they lacked in membership they made up in community strength. There were always activities buzzing within the church hallways—from Bible studies to potlucks, concerts with the Hidden Creek Carillon League to book clubs. The church was a center of life.

"Let's pray." Father Leo held Susan's hands. "Father of all mercies, strengthen your servant Susan as she navigates the wilderness of recovery. Be an anchor for her soul in rough waters. Guide her steps. Give her insight and understanding in your peace and divine love. She is broken and hurt; turn grief into joy. Relieve her burden with a heart of faith and love. With calm expectancy, may she rely on your perpetual power to heal, accept your healing gifts. Fill her with a confidence of faith and the courage of hope. In the turbulent unrest of loss, may she gain an awareness of your understanding."

"Amen." The prayer instantly brought peace to Susan.

"It is not an easy thing to lose a spouse, especially when betrayal lurks in the shadows. It tears at the soul and embitters the mind, confusing direction. You are lost in loneliness, anger, betrayal, regret, guilt…" Father Leo counseled.

"You can add *fear* to the list." Susan sighed.

"You are grieving, grieving the loss of your husband and the life you shared. You are also grieving the loss of trust. It is hard to trust yourself, let alone anyone else, when you have been deceived. Bradley, for better and for worse, loved and hurt you. The adage says you shouldn't speak ill of the dead. That is true to a point. It is God's jurisdiction to judge the sinner's actions. It is our duty to forgive Bradley, praying his soul may be relieved from the burden of the sins he carried through the grace of Jesus Christ. Bradley has his own healing process to go through on the other side. Sin leaves a muddy sediment only God can wipe clean." Father Leo paused. "While it isn't healthy to cling to the anger of betrayal, you cannot bury the rage either. So, speak ill of Bradley, fluidly express every nuance of emotions. Be honest. I want you to write down every thought about Bradley Dixon running through your mind in the next two minutes."

Susan flooded the paper with her emotions, writing down word after emotional word:

Anger, outrage, exasperation, desperation, pain, longing, confusion, husband, betrayer, turmoil, unrest, broken, burned, unfaithful, liar, con artist, hurting, sadness, unquenchable sorrow, weakness, fool, regret, reckless, turbulence, blurry, desire, frustration, love, loneliness, abandonment, fear, desolation, misunderstanding, debt, rage, hope, lost without him...

"Time's up." Father Leo pulled the paper away from Susan. "Judging from this list, you are experiencing a range of viable and potent emotions."

"I am angry at him; I don't understand how the man I loved could treat me with such cruel abandon. It isn't fair." Susan relinquished her tears, allowing the salt and water to flood from her eyes.

"It isn't fair. The age-old curiosity and biggest stumbling block in our road to faith is "Why do we suffer?" Surely the all-loving and compassionate God we rely on cannot be so cruel? We lash out, cursing him for the pain. I then remember that God sent his only son, Jesus Christ, to suffer amongst us. To bear the burden of pain and suffering, death, on the cross. He raised up his son from the dead to be a living hope and a sure foundation. Darkness cannot seize the light of Christ. Through suffering comes healing. Christ understands our suffering; he suffered in the flesh during his sojourn in the world. He feels our every emotion, from joy to anger. God is with us always, sharing the hurt in our hearts. He feeds you with the sustaining spirit of his presence to lead you through darkness into a new peace. The road isn't meant to be easy. Not because you are being punished, but because the situation isn't easy. It takes time to peel back every layer of complex emotion. An open wound needs to heal before it can become a scar."

"I'm a shadow of myself, broken and fragmented. I'm shattered, like glass. Every time I try to pick up the pieces, I cut myself on another memory, or a splinter of anger reopens the wound. I'm bleeding out, wounded and flightless."

"Be open to the pain of your heart; God enters through the brokenness. Let God's light burst through the storm clouds that hover over you and renew you in hope. It might just be a small glimmer of light, a minute patch of blue sky, but that is the first step. Pray for patience. Accept patience. Grieving is not a one-stop quick fix. It takes time. In the early stages of grief, you experience shock, a numbness swells up such that you cannot cope with the pain."

"That's how I felt the night of Bradley's death. A part of me is still in shock."

"You yearn for answers and search for understanding." Father Leo empathized

"Questions constantly rattle my brain. Why did my husband die in that car crash? Did he ever love me? Was our relationship a lie? It's an interconnected web of confusion. I've nearly uncovered the truth only for it to escape my clutches. I seesaw between the desire for information and the reconciliation that I will never understand why my husband died and why he left me with such hardship. It's an enigma that stifles the mind and agitates the heart."

"In the search for understanding, there are periods of disorganization and despair. A willingness to control and let go. You think that you have cleared this hurdle, optimistically reorganizing your life, only to trip over a nearly forgotten memory, cutting yourself on glass. It's okay to take two steps forward and one step back. I would not be surprised if at times you wrestle all the steps in the grieving process concurrently. Allow yourself time to grieve. When you feel vacant, a shell of your former shelf...let God fill the void, with his all-encompassing compassion. He will bind your wounds in His mercy and love."

"Everyone tells me I can't live in the past, yet I'm chained to it. Deciphering the memories, searching for clues…desperate for answers."

"You cannot be chained to the past. On the other hand, ignoring your history will only lead to problems in the future. The past is still your present because you have not healed from past wounds yet. So yes, let go—to truly let go is to cut ties without regret, to have that peace in letting go. Forgiveness is at the core of the healing process. You must forgive yourself and in time forgive your husband."

"I pray he is in heaven—at peace. Despite everything, I think he was a decent person, albeit horribly flawed. Still, I hold too much pain and anguish to forget what he's done."

"Forgiveness is not letting the person off the hook. It isn't dismissing the sin as much as having mercy on the sinner. Forgiveness is an act of your will, a choice to detach from revenge and hopelessness and to embrace faith and hope in the spirit of Christ. Focus less on your right to harbor hate, and more on God's command to forgive as he has forgiven us. Forgiveness cleanses you from the burden of anger. It allows you to move forward. In my experience, forgiveness isn't an instant epiphany, a lightning-flash cure. Forgiveness is an evolutionary process. It takes time to process the pain, releasing the anger layer by layer. You make the choice to forgive, but oftentimes the process of forgiveness takes a while—because you have to work through the emotional upheaval, close the open wounds. Sometimes you think you have moved on only for the anger to burn again, but each time you deal with the memory it is easier to forgive."

"It's hard to let go when I'm constantly bombarded with reminders of my husband's deceit. My retirement is depleted. I'm living in a ninety-year-old cabin, alone and scared. I'm afraid."

"Fear is a dangerous emotion. It is the antithesis of love; fear possesses a dark negative power to break us. It leaves you fragmented while the love of God makes us whole. Fear is not a virtue. Petition Our Father to replace fear with faith, anxiety with peace, distrust with trust, and loss with hope. For every fear that riddles your mind and poisons your heart, say 'Fear Not.' This expression is used 365 times in the Bible. God does not want us to fear, he wants us to go confidently before him in faith with trust that he can and will provide and heal us."

"It's hard to 'fear not' when you straddle the brink of disaster and have to start over."

"Life is full of transitions, beginnings, and endings. The sun rises and the sun sets, and hurries back to where it rises. You are starting over. Start—it is a positive word. You must deal with the mess left behind, but you can turn your weeping into joy. The heart of this arrow is betrayal. The weapon of betrayal was financial deprivation. Pray for the grace to see money and possessions in the light that God wants you to see them—as gifts. Money and temporal stability can never replace the provision and satisfaction that God's love can provide. This doesn't mean that you don't face the reality of the situation. You are being forced to start over with a new job and to rebuild your savings—it's a scary time. Trust that God will provide for you on earth and with the covenant promise of everlasting life in his glory."

"I'm torn between bottling in my fears and screaming out for help. Life is on autopilot; my soul is disconnected."

"Fear paralyzes. Faith in Christ's love and forgiveness teaches us to fly, so that we may soar. Worry is an ever-present emotion in the heart of every creature. In times of trial, we often fall into worry as a crutch. We analyze problems through the cloud and fear of that worry. I struggle with this daily. Worry doesn't enable us to escape a situation, it makes us unfit to cope with trials. While storms engulf us, don't stand in the rain worrying about lightning—instead, seek shelter in the Lord. He will give you the discernment, understanding, and tools to rise above difficulties. He will comfort you."

"I struggle to turn over my fear and anxiety to God. When I do, it's a piecemeal process, a superficial recognition that I can't control my situation. I keep analyzing, stuck in an unsearchable web of the pain, anger, desire for retribution. I seek answers. I cloak myself in worry. The past haunts the present. I fear the future, be it finances, loneliness, the ability to trust again."

"Proverbs 3:5–6." Father Leo opened the Bible, asking Susan to read the verse aloud.

"'Trust in the Lord with all thine heart; and lean not on thine own understanding. In all acknowledge Him, and he shall direct thy paths.'"

"Trust, once broken, splinters like burned wood. It is prickly and harsh—just when you think you can trust again, it pierces the skin."

"Once burned…"

"In turmoil, when a storm rages, instinct tells us that trust is a false friend. Don't lose heart. God proves his trustworthiness time and time again; throughout the scriptures, history, and in our own lives, his spirit is at work within us. The verse from Proverbs is not saying that we shouldn't use our minds that God has blessed us with, but that our wisdom is flawed and pales in comparison to God's wisdom and truth. By relinquishing the control of fear that you cling to, submitting worry to God, he will make you truly self-reliant, helping you to move forward, not restrained by bygone history, free to embark into an open future of promise."

"I have confidence in God's trustworthiness. The problem is that I don't trust myself."

"God will guide you through that process. His healing and restoration are available, but you must choose by your own volition to petition God to step in to reap the benefits. Open the floodgates to let his healing waters cleanse you. He will break apart the clouds and through your choice to follow him, you will be made whole. Trust, faith, and healing…" Father Leo flipped to another verse. "Hebrews 11:1, 'Now faith is the substance of things hoped for, the evidence of things not seen.' Faith is perceiving as real that which is not revealed to the senses and trusting that God who formed the world out of nothing, carving a piece of himself so that we may live, will break the darkness. Hope referenced in Hebrews isn't English vernacular. You can hope that you win the lottery; that is something that could come to pass but is not rooted in promise. Hope in the Christian context is trust that hope and faith in God will heal and reveal truth, understanding, and the grace of eternal life. See hope in Christ as a guidepost, not an uncertain wish for the future. In our Christian faith we must be risk-takers, not blind, out open to the guiding light of the spirit. It is something that comes from the core depths of our souls that only we can act on. It is not zealous rage."

"My dad always said that when you're driving on a road and reach a crossroads, remember Christ at this junction. A crossroads can confuse and confound. Which way do we go? Think of the cross. Christ suffered before the glory of heaven could be revealed. We have to cross barriers to break through."

"Kip Blanchard was a wise man. Hold close to his sound advice."

"I was offered a job at the Solitude Lake Lodge," Susan revealed.

"The extra money will alleviate financial worry, while the interaction with co-workers and guests will be good interaction. The trick is don't overdo it. In the grieving process you need to balance staying busy and finding solitude. If you try to avoid the reflection process, throwing yourself into work and activities, you won't heal. That is a masking and false coping mechanism," Father Leo advised.

"I want solitude," Susan whispered.

"Not to bombard you with homework, but I have prepared a self-reflection study. It includes weekly lessons, articles, and devotionals to help you through your process of discovery. I also want you to start a daily journal, honestly documenting your emotions and chronicling the process of grief and healing. I've taken the liberty to sign you up for a retreat in Bigfork at Rock Haven Camp the second weekend of September."

"Retreat?" Susan had shied away from interpersonal grief and survivors' groups. She'd never felt comfortable sharing her so-called dirty laundry.

"Angela Meyer, a renowned psychiatrist and grief counselor out of Kalispell, is organizing the weekend. You'll have the opportunity to participate in a few lectures, workshops, and therapy sessions, as well as time to relax. The retreat is centered on those surviving a crisis, be it a death in the family, overcoming addiction, domestic abuse, loss…"

"It sounds daunting," Susan said, blunt in her hesitation.

"You have to climb mountains to see the view. This retreat, coupled with the study I've compiled for you, will be worth the effort."

"No time like the present to start hiking, I suppose."

Chapter 9

"You did what?" Molly Arnett's face was on fire.

"I hired Susan Dixon to be our new Children's Activity Coordinator." Keeley shrugged.

"I'm the owner of the lodge. It is your duty to consult with me on new hires."

"Susan is not a new hire. Her great-grandfather designed the lodge, putting his signature mountain style into every stone, log, and beam. Susan spent six years of her life, from ages sixteen to twenty-two, working at the lodge. She is a former employee, neighbor, and a friend."

"You know how I feel about Susan being back in Hidden Creek."

"I know that we need to fill this position by May 28. Susan is a certified teacher with vast experience in the field. She's the perfect fit for this job."

"I don't question her qualifications," Molly huffed. "Don't you see what this will do to Jake? How he'll latch on to her?"

"Is that such a bad thing? If you recall, Jake is at fault here. He never would admit that he loved Susan when he had the chance. He shouldn't have been surprised when Bradley Dixon came along and swept her off her feet Susan told Jake point-blank, 'If you don't want me to marry Bradley, then I won't,' and Jake gave his blessing."

"I do not need a history lesson."

"Then why take Jake's foolishness out on Susan? She's suffering right now. Her life has been torn apart. She needs a summer job; more importantly, it's vital to our business that we hire her. Children's activities are essential to the lifeblood of the lodge. Families rely on the services we provide. Susan has the passion and professionalism to get the job done. Hire Susan or we'll be forced to cancel children's activities—it's that simple."

"I'll need to interview her before I can consider a final offer," Molly said, finally caving.

"Don't be ridiculous," Keeley said firmly. "She'll be here tomorrow morning at ten o'clock, to discuss details."

"What's all the shouting about?" Walter Arnett, a giant of a man at six foot seven, entered the conversation.

"Our daughter has been foolish enough to offer Susan Dixon the Children's Activity Coordinator position."

"Sounds more like a stroke of genius if you ask me, darling." Walter kissed his wife on the cheek.

"What about Jake? How will he handle the pain of working with Susan day after day?"

"Jake is a grown man and Susan is more than qualified for the position. She's a gem of a girl, and if our son can't handle having her around, it's his dilemma alone," Walter held. "The worst that could happen is nothing at all. I for one would like to see Jake and Susan reconnect as friends...or something more substantial."

"What is everyone yabbering about?" Gilligan came in from the boathouse. Named after his great-grandfather, Gilligan oversaw sailing and boating at the lodge. His job title had made him the scrutiny of more than a few *Gilligan's Island* jokes. Like his brothers, he was ruggedly handsome, with mysterious hazel eyes and chiseled features.

"Susan Dixon is going to work at the lodge this summer." Molly pressed her lips together, dramatically showing her disdain.

"That is great news," Gilligan said, immune to the controversy.

"Great news," Molly muttered, beyond frustrated. "For the record, she isn't hired yet."

Susan wrestled with nightmares, her anxious mind rapt. She woke up screaming like a rabid dog after a vision of Bradley's accident. Cold and sweaty, she rose from the bed, realizing that sleep was a futile attempt at this point. She made her way to the kitchen and brewed a pot of Constant Comment tea.

Layered in a fleece jacket and wool scarf, she carried her thermos and devotional materials to the back deck. An hour before dawn, the stars remained scattered with the moonlight glowing above the water. The pitch-black night had warmed to an effervescent blue. Susan sat, rocking in her iron chair, her mind void of thoughts except the approaching sunrise.

A flicker of red, a signal fire, warmed behind the mountains as the chirping of birds whispered morning. One could never be fully prepared for the intensity of a Western sunrise—it awed with intense color as light peered over the mountains. The cold breath of frost still hung in the air as the comfort of the sun broke down the darkness—purples, pinks, oranges colliding into a symphony of color. Then the sun emerged over the peek, raging with a brightness that flooded the earth, the lake sparkling, golden.

In the distance, the haunting call of the loon rushed over the water. The birds wandering, paddling on their aquatic home—Solitude Lake.

"The cry of the loon, so peaceful, haunting, and lonely. Strange how their fear stirs them to abandon their young if disturbed in their habitat..." Somehow the battles in the natural world brought Susan to a new peace, if only for a moment. She too had experienced the fear of the loon, where you would run, forsaking what you cared about because you couldn't face the unknown. Yet, all that does is leave promise behind.

Susan opened her devotional binder. Father Leo had put a lot of time and effort into the course, for which she was grateful. The first week's readings focusing on Psalm 30, Matthew 8–9, and Hebrews Chapter 11, with specific verses and topic discussions for each day.

As Susan read the first verses of Matthew 8, she realized the relevance of the scripture.

"And behold, a leper came to him and knelt before him, saying, 'Lord, if you will, you can make me clean.' And Jesus stretched out his hand and touched him, saying, 'I will; be clean.' And immediately his leprosy was cleansed."

She rested on the words. A leper was diseased, his skin afflicted, and soul tired. Though her physical body was not cursed with disease, her heart was sick. She needed healing. Lepers were outcasts, deemed unclean and forsaken. She'd been abandoned. Lepers were scorned, by society as well as their own anxiety and fear most hiding in the shadows, having given up their chance to be healed.

Yet in this encounter the leper, bogged down by circumstances, rose boldly in faith to seek Jesus. The leper humbly asked for help, with confident hope that Jesus would heal him. The leper didn't question Jesus's ability to heal, only asked that he heal the afflicted, if it was his choice. Jesus stretched out his compassionate love and quickly said, "I will; be clean."

Susan felt exposed, covered in the grime of circumstances, the weight of Bradley's mistakes and her own fears breaking her down.

If she could just muster the courage to ask Christ for his healing, he would give it to her...perhaps with instant precision, but more likely he'd give her the strength to let go of the hurt and allow healing to take place.

Several hours of solitude, prayer, and contemplation had certainly buffered Susan's morale. She fixed a late breakfast of eggs and toast before prepping for her appointment at the Solitude Lake Lodge.

She oscillated like a pendulum, contemplating the job offer. The Solitude Lake Lodge. Images of past summers, childhood memories, joy, and heartache inundated her thoughts. The memories of sandy shores, hiking with Jake, and swim lessons made her smile. Then there were the shadow thoughts, convoluted fragments of love and hate, frustration and bitterness, from her father's sudden death, to meeting and falling in love with Bradley Dixon. Could she stand a chance working at a place with so many ghosts? Could swimming in the shelter of its deep unstable waters heal the jaggedness inside, or would the dead weight cause Susan to drown?

Finishing the last of her toast, she recalled her first encounter with Bradley. Susan was on the cusp of sixteen. Her dad was still alive. It was the second week of June, and the air was hot. Summer had arrived at Hidden Creek. Susan was working as a lifeguard at the public beach in addition to her job as a waitress at the lodge. It was a Saturday, and the beach was crowded with locals and tourists.

The hot topic of conversation among the beach staff was Hidden Creek's newest citizen, Bradley Dixon. The teenage girls were gushing over the handsome stranger. Susan, on the other hand, paid Bradley no mind. At that time her heart was tied up in knots. She had grown accustomed to thinking that boys like Bradley Dixon would pass her by in exchange for thin and perfect beauties like Meredith Woods or gorgeous Julia Roberts look-alike Kelly Saunders.

Meredith's outer beauty was scarred by her petty need to belittle those around her. Susan was a favorite target of Meredith's. At Missoula Prep, she'd played tricks on Susan in such vulgar fashion that it cannot be revisited in writing. That day was no different, Meredith plotting tricks to make fun of Susan, all the while trying to reel in the attention of new heartthrob Bradley Dixon. As Susan sat on the lifeguard tower, looking out at children and families swimming in the lake, Meredith, and her clique approached with Bradley in tow.

"Bradley, I'd like to introduce you to Suzy Blanchard. Don't let Suzy's size worry you, despite all that blubber, she is a whale of a swimmer. It really is a tribute that at her size she can sit on that tower without it collapsing," Meredith heckled.

At the time, Susan desired nothing more than for those twits to like her. She fasted for weeks before the summer swimsuit season in hopes that a few pounds off her hips would make her less the pawn of jokes. In truth, Susan was healthy— she was muscular and athletic. Still, she couldn't accept the fact that she didn't look like the so-called popular girls at school.

Susan had tried to ignore their snotty comments, instead politely saying, "Hello." On the surface, Bradley seemed friendly enough, although she distrusted him. It was a vile trick. Perhaps her first instincts had been right all along.

"Are you going to the dance at the lodge tonight?" Meredith pressed Susan.

"Yes," she stammered.

"Bradley has agreed to take me," Meredith boasted. "It's a shame that no boy in town would ever dream of asking you to dance. I've tried to convince the boys you're a charity case, but no one will budge."

"For the record, I am going to the dance. With Jake Arnett."

"Jake sees you as his little sister. That's why he takes such pity on you."

"Enough chitchat—let's go swimming," Bradley pressed Meredith.

"If you insist." Meredith kissed Bradley on the cheek. He didn't seem to appreciate the gesture.

"It was nice to meet you, Susan," he stated in a moment of sincerity before running off with the "twit brigade" and jumping into the water

It was less than ten minutes later when Susan noticed that Bradley was struggling to swim, screaming for help. Without hesitation, her lifeguard instincts kicked in. Susan jumped down from the tower. She raced to the water and swam to Bradley's aide.

After pulling him to shore, Susan did CPR until Bradley coughed up water and opened his eyes.

"Thank you for saving me, Susan."

Susan's heroics shut Meredith and the rest of her gang up for the rest of the summer. An article in the *Hidden Creek Gazette* featured Susan's swimming accomplishments and talent as a lifeguard. Bradley and Susan became close friends after the incident. He started working at the Solitude Lake Lodge, with her and Jake. The pair became close friends that summer.

In retrospect, Susan often wondered if Bradley had staged the near drowning. She knew him to be a stellar athlete and fish in water. It was that sort of kindness, to set aside his ego to help a bullied teen shine, just for a moment, that led Susan to fall in love with Bradley. It made it all the harder to understand how a man so compassionate and caring could turn so reckless and spiteful. Had it all been a ruse?

Dabbing on Chap Stick and sunscreen, she composed herself. Memories be darned, she needed a job and the lodge fit the bill perfectly.

"Here we go…" Susan got into her car and drove the few miles to the Solitude Lake Lodge.

Susan's heart pounded as she stepped into the beautiful building. The atmosphere of the lodge's rustic majesty instantly tugged at her heartstrings. She slipped into the history and mystery of the stone, mortar, and ancient wood. Whispers of the past and future colliding.

The architecture inspired a subtle spell, casting one to search the ceilings of hand-hewn log beams and high rafters, where a grand and spiral log staircase climbed to the second floor and on to the rickety yet stable crow's nest.

A grand fireplace, cackling with embers and smelling of rich cedar, filled the room. The décor, charming and elegant without being ostentatious, was reminiscent of alpine chalets mixed with turn-of-the-century hunting lodge. Oriental rugs and Native American tapestries lined the hardwood floors. Comfortable sitting nooks and conversation areas were scattered in the lobby while an art-deco Western-infused reservation desk stood below a giant copper clock.

The grand lobby was connected to the first-story lodge rooms via a "secret passageway," while steps and an antique, fully operational elevator took guests upstairs, where hidden reading spots and desks were positioned. The lobby opened to the Whistling Elk Saloon and Solitude Dining Room on the left.

The Whistling Elk was the ideal spot to toast a good day's fishing. It had personality and decades of character. Charles Lindbergh, C.M. Russell, and A.B. Guthrie were just a select few of the notables to have sat at the oak bar. It was a popular haunt for nearby residents, including fishermen, hunters, ranchers, and tourists…making for a colorful history, not to mention rumors of a ghost or two (notably Whiskey Jack). The bar was equipped with a fireplace, cozy seating, and stark bar stools. It was much noisier than the neighboring dining room.

The dining room offered stunning views of the lake. Boaters could dock in the small marina just outside the restaurant and come in for a hearty, gourmet feast. The restaurant boasted a five-star chef, Aaron Hartman, and had been featured in numerous travel magazines. The restaurant's philosophy was organic, local Montana food with an international edge. The menu spanned from bison burgers and fine cuts of Montana-raised grass-fed beef to trout and salmon, to fusion-inspired dishes and local game. The wine list featured local favorites such as Mission Mountain Winery and Flathead Cherry wine, in addition to merlots and chardonnays from the Columbia Valley as far south as Argentina.

"Hello," Susan called out as she searched the property for Keeley. Instead, she was greeted by Molly Arnett.

"Ms. Dixon." Molly surveyed Susan. She was just as beautiful, if not more so, than when she'd worked at the lodge over fifteen years ago. Yet, age, perhaps the turmoil of her current circumstances, had left a slight, albeit visible, blemish on Susan.

"Mrs. Arnett, it is wonderful to see you." Growing up, Susan considered Molly Arnett as her second mother. Yet in the past decade, Molly had grown distant and cold in her dealings with Susan. Susan never fully understood why, although she guessed it had to do with Jake's dislike of Bradley.

"You've known me since your birth—please call me Molly. Mrs. Arnett makes me feel old."

"You haven't changed, still young and fiery as always." Susan smiled.

"I'm afraid Keeley misspoke when she offered you the Children's Activity Coordinator position." Molly cut to the chase.

"Oh?" Susan's heart sank.

"Don't fret, you're still the front-runner. It's procedure that I interview applicants prior to their hiring."

"I understand. I can provide you with my résumé and references?"

"Don't be ridiculous. I know that you possess a keen talent with children and are a hard worker. I also know that you're traversing a difficult patch right now. Your heart is fragile."

"If you're worried about my emotional state, I can assure you that I'm up for the job. I need to work."

"Jake mentioned you're having dinner tomorrow?"

Susan gulped.

"Nothing formal, just a casserole dinner at the Lone Moose. I'm eager to catch up. Jake and I were best friends growing up…then I moved to Seattle, and we lost touch."

"You got married." Molly sighed pointedly. "I am sorry about Bradley's death. It confounds me how he could leave you in such a wretched spot. I suppose he had more of his father in him than we all realized."

The statement made Susan uncomfortable, dividing her sentiments. She had often questioned Bradley's DNA. Had his father's influence been so maliciously strong that her husband couldn't escape it? Had Bradley chosen to give in to the cursed hate his father lived by? Or was Bradley confused and weathered? Did he mean to hurt Susan, or had that been a secondary effect? As much anger as she harbored for Bradley, she didn't like bashing his character. There were too many questions and complex layers in the ghost of Bradley Dixon to understand and reconcile against shadow and light.

"I take solace in the fact that God never gives us more than we can handle. I'm blessed to call the Lone Moose home."

"The Children's Activity Coordinator position is one of the most critical roles at the lodge. We're a family resort, so it's crucial that we offer activities that are fun and engaging. Nature programs, arts and crafts, water recreation…these are just a few of the daily activities we offer."

"I have great ideas for the summer program that will engage our campers." Susan handed Molly her proposal for creative activities for the lodge children's program. Susan's passion for teaching and interacting with young minds was fuel for her soul.

"You always had a creative mind." Molly's tone was evasive. She remained internally conflicted about the hire. She had to admit that Susan's ideas and enthusiasm made her a compelling candidate. "I need to speak with my husband first. I'll let you know by Thursday if we can take you on."

"I want this job. You won't be disappointed if you hire me."

Molly knew that it was fruitless to keep Susan away from the lodge; she'd always held some sort of otherworldly connection to the lake and the lodge. Susan would be a strong hire, much loved by guests. Molly just prayed that Jake's love for his old flame wouldn't burn into an uncontrollable wildfire.

Chapter 10

Pots, pans, measuring cups, mixing bowls, spoons, and recipe cards littered the Lone Moose kitchen, leaving it an organized mess. Susan couldn't remember the last time she'd entertained a dinner guest.

An amateur chef with a passion for cooking, it felt good to be back in the kitchen, the aroma of spices, sizzle of the skillet, and rush of experimenting with flavors. She hoped that her hard work in the kitchen would yield a savory feast.

She finished her brisket casserole, sweet potato soufflé, and flan before noon. Susan was due in town at the Thistle & Vine Tea Room to meet with Hidden Springs High School's principal, Marjorie Hatfield, at one o'clock.

She would then drop off the latest round of donations at the library and thrift shop, before picking up her mail at the post office, paying her energy bill, and finally stopping by Mystic Outfitters for propane, tarps, and other summer recreational supplies.

The weather had warmed significantly in the past week to a balmy seventy degrees. The cerulean sky, vast and open, stirred an ocean of possibilities in Susan's soul. She couldn't help but fret about the job at the lodge. Molly's standoffish behavior annoyed Susan. She'd served the lodge for six loyal years of her life; the Arnetts and Blanchards were intertwined like family. What rift had occurred for Molly to be skeptical of Susan's capabilities? It puzzled her.

Thistle & Vine was a quirky tearoom in a Frank Lloyd Wright–style bungalow just off Front Street. Meg Perkins and her sister Francesca Cummings had purchased the house seven years earlier, restoring the dilapidated edifice to its former glory. The tearoom featured a variety of pastries and over two hundred varieties of tea, including their signature Huckleberry Earl Grey blend.

"Welcome home." Marjorie embraced her friend and new hire. "It is a joy to have you joining the staff at Hidden Creek High in the fall."

"I enjoyed my tenure in elementary, but I am thrilled to delve into literature and history on the 11th and 12th grade levels. Hawthorne and Dickens cast a feverish spell over me."

"Here is the latest curriculum for next year."

'I look forward to reviewing the curriculum and building a strong academic program for the school year."

"I know you'll thrive molding young minds at HSH. How's the Lone Moose?"

"I'm abiding by the rules of the cabin…campfires, sunrises, and hiking."

"Any summer plans?"

"I'm looking forward to relaxing at the lake and preparing for the fall semester…and there is a chance that I'll serve as the Children's Activity Coordinator at the Solitude Lake Lodge."

"I can't think of a better person for the job."

The colleagues chatted about a variety of subjects over a pot of Glacier Spice Tea before parting ways at two o'clock.

"My husband, Lawrence, and I are planning a grill out on Sunday, sunshine or snow. We'd love to have you."

"I'll be there."

Susan spent the next few hours running errands around town: dropping off the latest round of discarded treasures, paying her electric and gas bills, and picking up and dropping off mail at the post office.

Hidden Creek's post office was an art deco building listed on the National Register of Historic Places. Susan loved the charm of the building. Door-to-door mail service wasn't available for Solitude Lake residents, so she'd have to make a weekly trip into Hidden Creek. The postal workers knew everyone by name, and the post office was a source of town news and the occasional gossip.

She capped off her errands with a trip to Mystic Outfitters, which was one of several shops in town specializing in recreational and angling gear. Mystic was owned by Keith Harriman, and they were the premier outfitter in town, specializing in guided fishing trips on nearby Mystic Lake and the Swan River.

From a young age, Susan had been taught the art of fly-fishing. Although she wasn't as graceful in her cast as her father had been, Susan had a keen touch as an angler.

"Blancher, you're back." Keith was a stocky gentleman of fifty-two with a grizzled beard. His wardrobe was always a variation of fishing shirts and angling vests combined with nylon outdoor pants.

"My rod is in a sorry state of disrepair. I'm hoping you can fix it?"

"I can sure try… I was sorry to hear about Bradley."

"Thanks." Susan brushed aside the topic. "It'd be great to get an update on the latest hatches, perhaps buy a few new flies to match with what's biting."

"I should be able to repair this rod back to its former glory in a few days," Keith assessed. "In the interim I can sort you out with new flies and line."

"Propane, fire starters, kindling, bug repellant, and tent pegs are just a few of the other items on my list."

"Planning to camp this summer?"

"I plan to get into the backcountry, if only for a night or two in an area campground." Susan's mind slipped to the Solitude Lake Lodge. If they hired her, it would be great to incorporate camping and fly-fishing 101 into summer camp activities.

"I'm planning a weeklong angling and backpacking trip up to Glacier National Park in July. Even splurging and staying a night at the Sperry Chalet, which is so remote you have to hike iand out.."

"Sounds exhilarating." Glacier National Park was located an hour and a half north of Hidden Creek. The town got a lot of tourist overflow from Glacier as visitors wound down MT 83 south en route to Bozeman and Yellowstone.

Settling her bill, Susan drove back to the Lone Moose. The dashboard clock in her Subaru read 4:10. She had just under three hours to change, put the finishing touches on dinner, and straighten up the house (or at least move enough boxes out of the living and dining room to eat a meal and have conversation).

Susan felt her nerves pinch as the clock ticked closer to her dinner date with Jake. They had a long and complicated history. Despite the fear of conjuring up sore memories, she looked forward to sharing a meal with the person who, despite time and bitter distance, she still considered her best friend.

Jake scrutinized his face in the mirror, his thick, wavy, disheveled hair, three-days-unshaven face, lonely green eyes, and chiseled jaw. He never paid much attention to his appearance. He was handsome, though he would never admit it. He was too busy putting sweat into keeping the lodge in order. Today felt different, though. He ran the razor blade down his prickly face, bleeding at the chin. He ironed his shirt and put on a pair of khakis.

Stubborn, he wouldn't openly admit that Susan Blanchard still cast a spell over him. She was under his skin. It made him angry, to a point that she unknowingly controlled him in such a way. But his love was too strong to hate her. After all, it was his own fault for losing her.

He braced himself. This dinner served as a step towards rebuilding his relationship with Susan, be it friendship or romance. Given the chance, Jake would have married Susan tomorrow. It was hard for him to realize that Susan's views of their relationship were staggeringly different. It was a friendship for her. She was still reeling from the death and betrayal of her husband. While Jake didn't lament Bradley's death, he hated the impact it had on Susan.

"Off to dinner with Susan, then?" Molly asked, still conflicted. "If only you'd put this much effort into cleaning yourself up on a daily basis."

"I clean up well enough," Jake said, ignoring his mom's disapproval.

"I prepared some dinner rolls and a side dish of cabbage salad," Molly offered. "Send them to Susan with my regards… And while you're at it…you might as well pass along the fact that she's hired for the Children's Activity Coordinator position at the lodge."

Jake looked puzzled. It was the first he'd heard of the proposition.

"The job offer is enclosed in this envelope. It details scheduling, duties, salary…all the pertinent information."

Memories of bygone summers overwhelmed Jake as he grappled with the news.

"I'll be blunt. I know that you love her. Understand that she needs time to heal. I hired Susan because she is qualified for the job. Don't use this as an excuse to get your heart broken again."

"Jake."

Susan, a bit numb, stalled as she opened the door. As their eyes met, ever so briefly. In that fleeting second, time temporarily transported Susan back to a scene from their youth, the night that things changed between her and Jake. She remembered the night before she left Hidden Creek, in her twenty-second year…the rain a tempest as the storm clouds enveloped them. The air was electric, lightning, and raw energy.

"Are you going to let me in, or am I forced to fend for myself out here in the cold?" Jake's teased.

"Of course, come in." Susan's smile ignited a flame in Jake's heart as she ushered him inside. "I apologize for the mess. I'm still rifling through moving boxes."

Jake surveyed the cabin, his first time in the Lone Moose in fifteen years, although he'd made a point to drive by the haunt at least once a week.

Much like the lodge, the Lone Moose drew you with an unassuming charm—a magnetic pull. Walking into the foyer, the left wing of the cabin was comprised of the great room and dining and kitchen areas, with a loft space overhead that included a small library and extra sleeping bunks. The right wing of the cabin included two bedrooms, a study, and the laundry area.

Messy as it was, the great room's lure could not be ignored. With hand-hewn Native American rugs, Montana heritage furniture, and a large stone fireplace crackling with warmth…the space instantly made guests feel at home.

"Dinner smells delicious," Jake said, breathing in the scent of the feast filling the cabin.

"On the menu, brisket casserole and an assortment of scrumptious sides."

"All this effort for me?" Jake gave his signature half-smile.

"It isn't often I get to entertain my oldest and dearest friend."

"I'm not old."

"Keep telling yourself that, partner."

"Mom sends her best." Jake set down the signature dinner rolls and cabbage salad.

Susan's thoughts turned to the job. Was she hired? Either way, she decided it best not to mention it to Jake. She didn't want to spoil their evening.

"Give me the scoop. What's the latest in the life and times of Jake Arnett?"

"The usual." He shrugged.

"Come on, there's got to be *some* excitement in your life."

"The fact that you're back in town is exciting. It is wonderful to have you back at the lake. I've missed you."

"I've missed you too." Susan realized how much. Being with Jake felt like home.

The pair fell quickly into conversation, as if no time had passed between them, laughing and reminiscing over a bottle of wine and a hearty meal. It seemed strange that such a great divide had pried its way between them so many years ago.

"The past few weeks, I've been organizing old photos, scanning them onto my desktop." Jake pulled out a small, weathered photo album. "I compiled this album for you."

Nibbling on chocolate cobbler, the friends went through the album, photo by photo, recalling past escapades, trials, and triumphs.

"Remember this?" Jake pointed to a photo of the pair, aged nine, dressed in their church best.

"How could I forget?" Susan laughed in front of tears. "Your cousin Amy's wedding. What a beautiful disaster."

"Disaster is more like it. They insisted on having everything outdoors. Mom told them you can't trust the weather—Murphy's Law points to that. Still Amy insisted."

"The day started out in perfection. Blue sky, ideal temps, the peace of the lake, the decorations… It was a beautiful backdrop for a wedding," Susan recalled. "Amy's dress, vintage lace and satin…Frank in his tux…who ever thought that cowboy would get into a Sunday suit, let alone a tux…the string quartet…and that wedding cake—huckleberry cream with lemon filling…"

"That was before all hell broke loose. Within seconds of Amy and Frank saying their 'I dos,' the rumble of thunder shook the ground and the once blue sky turned an ominous black."

"At least the weather held off until they were pronounced husband and wife."

"Barely. The hail rained down from the sky the second they started kissing. The wind was so strong, it blew apart Amy's veil and sent it flying into the nearby water. Everyone rushed inside the lodge until the pounding hail stopped and the rain turned into a light drizzle. In typical Montana fashion, within a half hour the sun lifted through the clouds. Amy and Frank kept saying, 'Rain on your wedding day is good luck.' The wedding party rushed outside for the buffet dinner. The dilemma?"

"The bears." Susan burst out laughing. "It really is unfortunate that the cake, so elegant, was left out in the storm. Not only did the tent collapse in the hail, but that family of black bears came and ate the entire cake and wedding feast. Dad's anger burned. Always the conservationist, he kept saying, 'A fed bear is a dead bear.' He was angrier at the caterers for putting the bears at risk than the fact the wedding feast was destroyed."

"Thank goodness for pizza delivery. Luna's bison pizza was better than the chicken cordon bleu and salmon fritters any day…at least to nine-year-old me."

"Somehow Amy's bouquet managed to stay somewhat intact."

"Remember what you said when you caught it?"

"I was over the moon to have the flowers until I discovered that catching a bouquet means you're going to get married. I was terrified. I said if it were absolutely imperative that I get married, then…"

"We agreed to marry each other." Jake smiled. "I was a gentleman and gave you an engagement ring, straight from a Cracker Jack box."

"I still have it, tucked safely in my jewelry box."

"After all this time?"

"I never had the heart to get rid of it."

Jake leaned in, desperately wanting to kiss Susan. It took all his strength to restrain his desire.

"Amy and Frank are still happily married today. They got the worse part of better straight off the bat."

Jake figured it was time to shift the subject. "I have news. You're officially hired as the Children's Activity Coordinator for the summer season at the lodge."

"I'm thrilled." Susan embraced Jake with a celebratory hug. "I promise that I will uphold the code of the lodge and be the best coordinator possible."

"I have no doubt in your capabilities." Jake marinated on the fact that he would be spending an entire summer working with Susan. He smiled.

Chapter 11

"I've got to get outside." Susan stared at Solitude Lake from her kitchen. The radiant light and vast Montana sky begged exploration.

Rummaging through the hall closet, she pulled out a backpack, a bear bell, and a windbreaker. The backpack was old and weathered, but sturdy enough for any expedition. She stuffed the pack with her canteen of water, a ham sandwich, trail map, camera, daily devotional materials, and her journal.

The plan: to hike to Hidden Creek Falls, a three-mile backcountry hike through open forests, skirting rock ledges and Hidden Creek. The trail was moderate, gaining four hundred feet gradually, while offering stunning views of Solitude Lake and the Swan Range, unique geologic formations, and the majestic Hidden Creek Falls, one of eight waterfalls that cascaded down the rocky cliffs as Hidden Creek rambled towards Solitude Lake.

Susan's wardrobe was a display in the fine-tuned art of layering, with a short sleeve knit, lightweight windbreaker, and heavier fleece, waterproof pants, and hiking boots. The weather in Montana was constantly changing. May was notorious for its vacillating moods, its weather shifting like a pendulum from harsh wind and wet snow to intense sun with clear skies.

Expecting the trail to be muddy, she wore her slush-resistant Gore-Tex hiking boots and Columbia weatherproof pants. The reward for mucking it through the mud and ice would be a stunning view of Hidden Creek Falls, powered by a Zeus force of melting snow tumbling the cliff in raging splendor.

She inhaled the aroma of the forest, a sweet scent of cedar, pine, wildflowers, and damp air. The forest was soggy and unstable as mud, ice, and water loosened rocks and rotted wood planks. Despite the upheaval, the deep roots of the towering evergreens stood firm as anchors of the forest. Pine needles cracked, bristling underfoot, contrasted by the slush of the earth.

Susan took her time climbing up the trail, meandering in solitary rhythm as the path rose in elevation. Her breaths weakened as the air thinned from the elevation gain.

"It is going to take time for my lungs to adjust to high-altitude living. I'll have to train my body to compensate for the lack of oxygen." The deep breaths and panting pressed her to continue. It was an invigorating trial.

With each bend in the path, the forest opened, revealing a rocky ledge with expansive views of crystal blue, piercing Solitude Lake and the rugged snowcapped Swans in the distance. This fairytale scenery defied the most vivid imagination. So stunning, so sharp, so raw, and so magical.

It was an hour trek to reach the falls, which were truly "hidden." The trail, traversing a meadow, without even a trickle of water, abruptly revealed the splendor of Hidden Falls.

Susan stood in awe as the waters of Hidden Creek flooded down forty feet with unbridled intensity. The gushing water plummeted from an ancient rocky edifice into a cavern below. To take one step farther than the edge of the trail, one could slip into the abyss. Yet standing on the precipice of its thunderous glory, one was moved to hope and inspiration.

A picnic table was set up in the vicinity of the falls, with a strict "pack in, pack out" notice. This was bear country, with the largest grizzly population in the Pacific Northwest inhabiting these forests.

Susan's father had taught her to respect the creature's might, never to underestimate its power. Living in bear country also taught Susan that all creatures, including the mighty grizzly, could have fragile strength. The bears had unique personalities and virtues. Despite their grizzled might, they also had the capacity for fear...they feared humans, death, hunger, and abandonment. Susan respected bears' grizzled grit and unassailable will to survive, navigating the wild in search of peace during conflict. All life was in search of understanding and survival in a world of death and miscommunication.

Susan avoided bears, knowing they deserved peace and respect—not because they were evil creatures, just a different species with hopes and fears that if provoked would attack.

After eating her sandwich, Susan dug into her daily devotional, reflecting on Jesus's power to heal the brokenhearted and bind their wounds.

Susan reflected on the word *bind*: binding a wound—what did it mean spiritually? She was bound by the misery of loss, but this binding was a binding of protection—a bandage to shield the heart.

"Lord, please bind my wounds. I am struggling."

Susan allowed herself to discover solitude in the scenery. She stared into the heart of the forest, the rhythm of the falling water fueled by freshly melting snow.

The falls felt like tears, breaking water. In the chaos of the falls, Susan discovered a precarious grace.

Susan wanted to be the water, strong, roaring without trepidation, yet she was caught in the brokenness of the rocks and drowning in the undertow of the rapids, unable to navigate. Instead of crying out for help, she tread ferociously in the white rapids to no avail. All she could do was barely keep her head above water.

Her limbs weak. Her mind tired. Her heart cold. Her fire burned with a flicker, an ember fading into darkness.

"I am lost and afraid. Heavy in burdens. I have no foundation to keep me from blowing away. My steps are broken. I stumble time and again. I lash out like the water's rage, but the river of my soul is a vortex, a black hole whirlpool only dragging me deeper into the abyss. I don't trust my own sense of self. My existence the past seventeen years was a lie, or was it?"

The Lord heals the brokenhearted and binds their wounds. The scripture nudged at her heart. Susan knew she needed to turn her pain over to God, but it wasn't easy.

This process would be long and tedious, yet if she could just relinquish a little bit of her burden to the Lord, day by day, and peel away the pain and joy of each memory, regaining trust with faith in his authority, Susan knew that his time of trial would not get the best of her.

In was in that moment of awakening that a doe, in such fragile grace, emerged from the forest, looking at Susan as a friend. It was striking, the animal so still and so intent. Both stood silently looking at one another at a distance. Then without warning the creature disappeared into the thick of the brush.

Chapter 12

The weeks leading up to the Memorial Day opening of the Solitude Lake Lodge moved at helter-skelter pace. Susan immersed herself in her new position, researching creative activities and fine-tuning the children's schedule.

The Lewis Center was the hub of children's programs. The cabin was an ideal hangout for youth. The space was equipped with board games, a television and DVD combo for movie nights, a kitchen, comfy sofas, bean bag chairs, and arts and crafts tables.

Dubbed the Solitude Explorers, the program incorporated natural scenery into the core camp activities, focusing on wilderness adventure, backcountry safety, hiking, learning how to build a tent and a fire, making s'mores, bird watching, swimming, zip-lining, canoeing, volleyball, naturalist programs, and young ranger events. The list of fun also included arts and crafts, games, scavenger hunts, photography, and fishing.

The program was divided into three age groups: the Young Buckaroos, ages 3–8, met weekday mornings, while the Lone Rangers, ages 9–12, and the Running Eagles, ages 13–18, met in the afternoons.

On Tuesday and Thursday nights, while parents enjoyed a quiet dinner in the lodge, children and teens were treated to stargazing, fireside storytelling, movie nights with pizza, board game play-offs, or even a camping trip (albeit in the safety net of a short walk from the main lodge to Discovery Campground).

The lodge was a hub for summer activities, offering a plethora of recreational activities and a jam-packed schedule of events, including the weekly barn dance and concert series. A daily guided hike to one of many regional trails was also a popular attraction.

The lodge's access to the pristine waters of Solitude Lake made it an ideal spot for water recreation. Emmett's Dockside Tack Shop was an *Orvis*-certified fly shop with licensed anglers on staff.

Water recreation included kayak, canoe, and sailboat rentals, swimming, water polo, and other fun ways to get your feet wet. Emmett's Dockside Tack Shop had resident angling experts on duty for daily guide trips.

On Mondays, the lodge played host to the Solitude Farmers Market, with local artisans, food vendors, and farmers. A portion of the proceeds went to a local nonprofit, while attendees from neighboring towns often rented kayaks or packed into the bar and restaurant.

Wednesday night programs included a campfire naturalist talk. The "fireside talks" ranged in topics from bats to bears, astronomy to geology, and Native American culture.

Friday nights the lodge hosted a Lakeside BBQ. The Saturday Square Dance was known throughout the region as the best place to move to the toe tapping sounds of the Hardscrabble Boys.

On Sunday, the week came to an end and began again with a nondenominational sunrise prayer service on the shores of Solitude Lake.

The lodge offered a variety of vacation packages, from weeklong all-inclusive escapes for the family, to one-night rentals. This dynamic atmosphere transported guests to a simple and refined solitude.

"Howdy stranger." Jake popped in to check on Susan's progress in the Lewis Center. "The Solitude Explorers program looks awesome. The itinerary for the first week makes me want to go back to summer camp—scavenger hunts, carnival crafts, bocce ball…"

"I am blessed to relive summer camp from a kid's perspective. It'll be a blast!" Susan paused; memories of countless summer days spent at the lake with Jake scrambling her mind. "How are things going on your end?"

"Everything is on track for the lodge opening."

"Keeley told me that Memorial Day weekend is sold out."

"Our reservations are booked solid through mid-July, with sparse openings in August and September."

"I'm looking forward to the Firemen's Dinner on Thursday."

The lodge had a fifty-year tradition of hosting a fundraising dinner for the Hidden Creek Fire Department the night before the lodge opened to the public. Tickets to the five-course meal were sixty dollars, with all funds going directly to firefighters.

"You've been working yourself silly. I think you can do with a siesta." Jake encouraged.

"I beg to differ."

"A girl has to eat. Why not throw a hike into the mix. An hour break tops."

"You're the one doing the heavy lifting. Molly won't be happy if I distract you from work."

"Gilligan is the one she has to worry about—I'm on target."

"I'll take a break on one condition," Susan relented.

"Anything."

"Lunch. I'm starving!"

The pair feasted on leftover roast beef and apple crisps in the employee dining room before trekking down the footpath on a picturesque stroll to Artist Point.

The trail ambled along the shores of Solitude Lake, revealing stunning panoramic vistas of the surrounding scenery, the glacier peaks of the Swan Range elegant and impenetrable. The water glistened underneath the deep blue sky, for a second resembling a diamond on fire.

Artist Point was a convergence of light and dark, a portal of magic and mystery converging into rugged simplicity. Its subtle complexities against the raw terrain of the Rockies made it a popular spot for watercolorists. Artist Point was in its glory on the cusp of night; it came alive at sunset, blazing in a tapestry of color and shadow.

Susan and Jake sat on driftwood on the shore, the water quietly lapping in the background. Counting their breaths, they inhaled the beauty of the place.

Jake found himself hooked in Susan's enigmatic green eyes. He pondered the thoughts occupying her mind.

"How are you?"

"Wonderful." Susan's smile was light and delicate. "This weather is extraordinary."

"I mean how are you coping with Bradley's death?"

"It has been difficult," Susan anxiously pushed back, avoiding the topic.

"I hate what he did to you," Jake whispered, afraid that if he spoke up his anger would tear the mountains down.

"It's a dead issue," Susan lied.

Susan would rather have her teeth pulled than discuss her dead husband with Jake. Jake and Bradley had been friends once. Their falling-out had been abrupt, harshly inflicting deep wounds. Susan owned up for playing a role in dissolving Jake and Bradley's relationship. The conflict was complicated and simple if you unraveled it. Both boys had claimed to love Susan. Jake refused to admit his feelings and Bradley got the girl.

"It's okay to be hurting. Pain is natural. You loved Bradley…" Jake struggled with words. "I'm here for you. Just say the word."

"I love my husband. I hate my husband. It's a struggle, but I will get through," Susan said, maintaining her composure.

"You're resilient. I don't doubt your ability to heal. Just know that I'm here for you. You are not alone."

"My husband died tragically. I might never fully come to terms with that trauma. Still, things are on the mend. I'm grateful for this job and the opportunity to spend the summer on the lake."

The conversation about Bradley ended as abruptly as it started. Even in death his ghost suffocated the air.

Dressed in a cocktail dress, black flats, and a scarf, Susan dabbled on muted red lipstick. She nearly put on mascara, but hesitated, afraid it might run, revealing the tears clinging to her eyes. It was the first time she'd been out to a semiformal event since Bradley's death.

The funeral. The church pews had been packed with friends and colleagues. There was one person strikingly absent: Ellis Dixon. Bradley and his father's contentious relationship had started on a collision course ten years back. Ellis expounded his dislike for Susan, casting her aside as a lowlife unworthy of his son. Ellis said if there wasn't a divorce he would never speak to Bradley, rejecting him as a son and heir. Ellis held Bradley's inheritance over his head as collateral, hoping money would sway his "wayward" flesh. Still Bradley remained committed to Susan and their relationship; at least, she thought he had.

Despite Ellis Dixon's cruelty towards his son, Susan had continued to reach out to him in the wake of Bradley's death. She felt that a father, even a lousy one, deserved some respect. Still Ellis had returned her letters unopened. She decided that she would reach out once more via certified mail. If he didn't respond, she would lay that burden to rest.

Is there rest in death? Susan recognized the paradox of the question as it weighed on her mind. Following his funeral in

Seattle, Bradley's ashes were moved to the columbarium at St. Michael's to rest in peace. And yet, Susan was restless.

Now that she was back in Hidden Creek, it seemed logical for Susan to grieve by visiting Bradley in the church graveyard, and yet she avoided it like the plague. The pain too deep and death too heavy to bear.

For all the unrest in her mind, Susan did look forward to the banquet. It would be an excellent opportunity to thank local firefighters for their service while also meeting and mingling with her new coworkers. Having Jake as her date would make the evening more bearable.

Over the past few weeks Susan and Jake had rekindled their friendship, old roots still strong. The pair spent spare minutes reminiscing about childhood over coffee. They hiked and fished after work, casting stones into the lake, watching the silent water ripple… Jake had always been a rock, solid and trustworthy. Together they were learning to trust again. Though ghosts of their past remained locked, out of focus, hidden out of sight.

Stepping into the Solitude Dining Room, Susan was drawn into the elegant décor of well-placed firefighter flags and fresh flower arrangements. Keeley had always had a knack for throwing a party. Her style rivaled Martha Stewart's but with a Montana flair. The ambiance of candlelight and light classical music invited guests to relax.

Lodge chef, Aaron Hartman, was a rising culinary star in the northwest. He'd designed a gourmet-meets-cowboy menu that would appeal to down-home firefighters in a home-cooked way. The five-course meal comprised of berry salad with vinaigrette accompanied by basil oregano hand rolls, hearty tomato soup, kokanee spring rolls, beef Wellington with asparagus, and a raspberry cheesecake for dessert. Big Sky wines and local ales fueled the libations.

"You dress up nice." Susan approached Jake, who looked handsome dressed in a freshly pressed suit and tie. His cowboy boots reminded her that he was a Montanan at heart.

"You always looking stunning."

"Don't make me blush."

"Glad you could make it." Gilligan and Russell entered the conversation.

Unlike their mother, Molly, Jake's brothers hoped that he and Susan would fall back in love. Gilligan remembered the summer fifteen years ago. Jake had always blamed Bradley for getting in the way of his life with Susan. Gilligan had a different perspective; his brother had foolishly pushed Susan, a girl who at the time desperately wanted Jake's love, into the hands of another man.

Jake and Susan were afraid to move past the façade of friendship, even though everyone around them could see they were attracted to each other.

Unfortunately, instead of trusting the spark, they both fought to cover the flame. Stubbornness had a habit of blocking paths. Susan had every right to marry Bradley. He was the one who courted her. When push came to shove, Bradley proposed, while Jake, fearful of rejection, retreated into a solitary life.

"I'm delighted to be part of this event. The Firemen's Banquet is the official beginning of summer on the lake." Susan enthused.

"It is a treat to have you working at the lodge again," Russell replied. "You have infused our children's program with a much-needed creative edge."

"I hardly consider it work to spend a summer on the lake enjoying games and outdoor excursions with children. I'm back at summer camp and it is a blast."

During the cocktail hour, Jake introduced Susan to members of the lodge staff. The lodge employed thirty-five souls each summer season, including waitstaff, kitchen crew, cooks, housekeepers, receptionists, fishing guides, trail guides, maintenance workers, lake staff, and more. Workers were mostly regional high school and college students, with a few seasonal employees hailing from as far east as North Carolina and Maine, and as far west as Alaska. The lodge season ran from Memorial Day to mid-October, depending on the snow.

"Blancher, I didn't know you were back at Solitude Lake." Fire Chief Mark Tomlin grew up two doors down from the pharmacy.

"I've moved into the Lone Moose on a permanent basis."

"No kidding?" Mark bit his lip. "I was sorry to hear about Bradley."

"Susan is working at the lodge this summer as the Children's Activity Coordinator. Just like old times," Jake noted.

"There's no better person for the job," Mark agreed. "Janet and I would love to have you over for dinner. The house has been empty since the twins left for Montana State."

"Drew and Brian are in college?" Susan gulped. It made her feel old, regretting that at age thirty-seven she was still childless. The chances of her having a baby now were slim. She certainly wasn't rushing back into romance with such emotional distrust left in the aftershock of Bradley's duplicity.

"I can hardly believe it myself. Drew is the academic, majoring in engineering, while Brian is a modern-day beatnik—moving from punk band to classical, music to film classes. They are a bit reckless at eighteen but have good heads on their shoulders. Both are working in Grand Teton National Park over the summer. I commend them for finding a way to get paid to fish and raft all day."

"Isn't it wonderful how Susan and Jake have reconnected?" Walt Arnett whispered to his wife as they sipped on Flathead Cherry wine.

"It's a disaster in the making," Molly said bluntly. "Don't get me wrong—I am grateful to have Susan on staff. Her program itinerary is the best we've had in years. I know that parents and kids will be thrilled with this summer's Solitude Explorers."

"I wish you weren't so hard on Suzy," Walt held. "She is a compassionate soul, who is bearing the brunt of a messy and toxic set of circumstances."

"I lament her current situation—it's tragic. Tragic, but not unexpected, when the likes of Bradley Dixon is concerned. He always was his father's son," Molly added, gritting her teeth. "I am not opposed to Susan and Jake rekindling their relationship. My fear is that Susan is rushing into romance with Jake as a coping mechanism. She's in the midst of a loss, a void you don't snap out of, and love on the rebound will break both their hearts. Jake and Susan both deserve better than a summer wildfire relationship that leaves them both burned and scarred."

"Molly, is it as dire as that? The kids were in love with each other long before Bradley came into the picture. If anything, Susan married Brad on the rebound when Jake rejected her."

"Don't worry, I'll hold my iron tongue. Our son's greatest asset and character flaw is the fact he is stubborn. My advice won't change his desire for Susan."

"Oh, Molly, let them be." Walt chuckled. "They both deserve a happy ending."

Chapter 13

The sun's brilliance radiated heat against virgin earth; the tepid dry swelled to an inviting seventy-three degrees. Summer whispered its song, heralding its victory over the retreating army of winter.

A fever of hope kindled inside Susan, her deepest gloom bathed in light, long days where the darkness of night was eclipsed by the stars—the entire galaxy in sight and the fullness of the moon. It was an unshakable feeling.

Her first week as coordinator was a huge success. The Solitude Explorers groups were well-behaved, enthusiastic kids, engaged in learning and adventure. The campers immersed themselves in a variety of activities, including an on-site camping experience, hiking, arts and crafts, and storytelling.

The lodge was aflutter with activity. The first farmer's market brought in close to five hundred people from as far as Bigfork and Missoula. Montana pottery, Native American artwork, homemade pies, alpaca wool, handmade purses, kettle corn, music, and more made for an entertaining night out. Susan used the opportunity to hand out flyers detailing children's activities, encouraging locals to sign up their kids for the Solitude Explorers program as day use. It wasn't a summer camp alternative as much as an excursion option for busy parents, to cater to their kids' energetic curiosity.

Jake and Susan volunteered to serve as hosts for the Friday night Lakeside BBQ. Dressed in cowboy attire, staff served up a buffet of bison brisket, organic pulled pork, and braised grilled chicken, along with corn on the cob, Montana toast, pinto beans, and sponge cake.

"I'm gaining ten pounds just looking at this mouthwatering food," Susan told Jake as they served guests hearty portions on cast-iron skillets.

"You've burned off zillions of calories this week chasing after kids, setting up camp, and kayaking. Besides, BBQ is worth the indulgence. It's a protein muscle build."

"True." Susan served herself. "It is invigorating, being back at the lodge. Solitude Lake is heaven on earth."

"Will you be at the square dance tomorrow?"

"I'm thinking about it."

"If you need a partner to dosey doe, I'm your cowboy."

"Me and my two left feet might take you up on that offer if you don't mind your feet getting kicked and bruised."

"Nonsense, you are the Ginger Rogers of the Swans."

"I'll take the compliment, even if you are blind to my faults."

After dinner, Susan and Jake picnicked by the docks, the range of pinkish and purple sunset hues reflecting off the lake.

"Stevie is pressing me to come to the rodeo at the ranch on Sunday. Can you spare the afternoon?"

"An afternoon of wrestling, wrangling, broncos, and barrel racing…count me in."

On Saturday morning, Susan hiked to Larch Point, a nature trailhead near the Lone Moose that led to a popular fishing hole. With her journal and devotional in hand, she let her mind wander. Looking into the soul of Solitude Lake, Susan's troubled and restless heart experienced a sudden catharsis as she released layer after layer of anger and frustration in the wild abandon. For the first time in months the distress that plagued her, her constant battle for answers, began to lift. She let go of a single splinter shard of pain, pain she clutched like a dagger prickling the skin.

Electricity kindling a friction of light in her soul, she found the will to live again, not just by breathing in air, but truly seeing life as a dynamic interaction with the world around her.

Her struggle with the past would persist, like a shadow, but its iron grip of darkness broke in the surging sunlight of her new life.

"I am going to embrace life and chase it down with wild hope."

After finishing her hike, Susan made her way to the lodge. She spent the afternoon leading the Solitude Explorers on a wildlife-themed scavenger hunt.

As the adventurous troop searched for treasure in the woods, Susan felt her own heart dance. She realized she too was on a scavenger hunt, discovering clues in the shadows of her past and reconciling them to a present she was trying to grasp. Each new clue gave her direction she could trek with bold hope into the future.

The Solitude Lake weekly square dance was the best little hoedown in the Swan Valley. Popular bluegrass and cowboy swing band the Hardscrabble Boys provided toe tapping beats, while Bob "Hollering" Whitey was a yee-haw caller. Whitey taught the dancers the steps with his Swan Valley sense of humor. The lodge dance incorporated traditional and Western square dances, as well as Western swing and cowboy waltzes.

Participants were encouraged to dress in colorful old-time apparel. Susan put on a pair of well-worn jeans and a ruffled shirt and vest, accompanied by her favorite pair of boots. Designed and handmade for Susan by Hidden Creek Boots & Hats, the boots were bright teal with a vivid diagonal pattern. She topped off her outfit with turquoise earrings and a silver cross necklace.

The square dance was held in the 1935 Red Barn. Recently remodeled, the barn had a state-of-the-art sound system, stage, and dance floor. The Square Kitchen Nook offered sweet treats and huckleberry cider for hungry dancers.

Susan let the atmosphere sweep her up as she remembered her first dance…her first dance with Jake decades ago.

The Hardscrabble Boys rosined their bows and tuned banjos, mandolins, and basses in preparation for the lively jigs to come.

Jake, donning a Stetson, faded jeans, and a button-down flannel shirt, spotted Susan as she entered the barn. He was struck with her beauty. Susan was not a common beauty, the type on a magazine cover that shocks you into admiration. Susan's beauty was deeper, it radiated an unassuming quality, that spark you can't put into words.

"Looking good, cowboy. Are you ready to swing and tap your toes on the barn floor?" Susan reeled Jake in with her smile. He had not seen her so carefree all summer.

"You bet your bottom dollar."

The dance kicked off just after eight o'clock, with the Montana Stomp melody.

"Swing your partner, round and round," Hollering Whitey shouted, calling out a series of steps. In the background, traditional folk melodies and cowboy rhythms kept the beat light.

The first set of dances were the more traditional Appalachian square dance and English Country dance, reels, and Montana contra dance.

A short break thirty minutes into the action gave dancers a chance to catch their breath over a cup of hot cider or hand-squeezed lemonade.

The next hour focused on a mix of line dances and waltzes, with traditional favorites "Goodbye Liza Jane," "Tennessee Waltz," "Ida Red" and ' Cotton-Eyed Joe."

Texas swing capped off the last thirty minutes as the Hardscrabble Boys fired up Bob Wills–inspired tunes. Jake and Susan found themselves paired off as the song "The Keeper of my Heart" began.

"'If again you were just mine, the sun for me would always shine…'"

"It's our song," Susan whispered. The pair used to dance to the ballad during their youth.

"'Though fate had ruled that we must part…'"

"We practiced for weeks to be ready for the big dance at school."

"'You're still the keeper of my heart…'"

"Our first dance."

A silent spell fell over the couple, lost in the music as they danced. Holding each other close, the moment a trigger igniting the spark. The burning passion of memories past clouding their perception. It was so easy to fall into one another's arms, yet so dangerous. Susan resisted passion that yearned to kiss Jake.

"I need some air." Susan rushed outside, her cheeks bright red.

"Are you okay?" Jake rushed after her.

"Fine. The heat of dancing just has me flustered suddenly." Susan's stomach fluttered. "I think I'm going to head home. Are we still on for the rodeo tomorrow?"

"'Looking forward to it."

With that, Jake and Susan parted, both wishing they could have held on to one another the rest of the night.

Chapter 14

Susan woke up dizzy, the previous night's dance fresh on her mind. She wrestled around her attraction to Jake, confused by rekindled feelings of passion. She tried to bury the spark between them in the recesses of her psyche.

"I am still grieving, I cannot get tangled up in a romance, especially with Jake. He's my best friend." Susan spoke firmly, trying to convince herself of the argument. She cared too much about Jake to twist his heart strings. Logic told her to put her foot down and tell Jake that they could only be just friends. Susan's emotions were far more muddled.

Susan found peace at church, where they celebrated Pentecost Sunday, the birthday of the Christian church. Father Leo gave an inspiring sermon focusing on the gift of the Holy Spirit.

"On Pentecost we commemorate the Holy Spirit's descent on the apostles, a visible and living testimony to the salvation of Christ and the gift of the Holy Spirit. The scripture from Acts describes a frenzied morning, in which the fire—power of the Holy Spirit—hit the tongues of apostles, who could in miraculous power speak in languages they did not know, breaking down communication walls to have the ability to testify to the truth of Christ's grace and the authority of the

Trinity. This communication, a reversal of the confusion of languages at Babel, demands that the Gospel of Christ is open to all, no matter their background. Willing hearts can receive the gift of the Holy Spirit. This was an active promise fulfilled—the Holy Spirit is God's gift to use, a connection with his love and guidance to fill our souls with sustaining fire.

"I proclaim Pentecost as an outpouring of hope, a stirring to repent and seek the savior who longs to fill our hearts. I entreat you to constantly seek the fulfilling force of the spirit. The choice to ask the Holy Spirit to fill your body, mind, and soul is a commitment of faith and love for Christ and the Father. It is a direct connection to the Father and his beloved son, Jesus.

"It is filling our cup with the outpouring of God's spirit into our very being. It renews us through baptism in the fire of the spirit and fills us with peace. Accepting the spirit is a startling journey of transformation, a freedom of conscience because of Christ's forgiveness. Christian freedom means to walk in the will of Christ, conducting oneself to the Holy Spirit's power and leading over our sinful flesh. The fire of the world is a fire that destroys. The fire of the Holy Spirit kindles our soul and sustains us in strife by faith.

"Resist. We push back the Holy Spirit. Humans don't like ceding over their independence. We like to cling to our misplaced sense of self, basking in our own self-centered importance, instinctively looking down on others and arguing that we can stand alone. Refusing the gift of hope and love leads to a dangerous imbalance in our lives—it is chaos. The Holy Spirit is the food we need to survive. It is like manna sustaining us in the spiritual and physical hungers of life. Love brings peace even in restlessness. Humans often choose to rebuke the promise and gift of love to fuel interpersonal tensions, planting the seeds of hate. Hate is a child of fear.

"Let go of the fear, relinquish your ego, and embrace the Holy Spirit. It is a gift, born out of God the Father and Christ's ceaseless love for us and longing for connection. The seven gifts of the Holy Spirit give us a road map to guide us through life's tribulations and reminds us not to lean on our own understanding but the authority and light of the Trinity.

"Come, Holy Spirit, fill the hearts of thy faithful and enkindle them in the fire of thy love. The gifts of the Holy Spirit are practical and fulfilling.

"Walk by the Spirit, and you will not gratify the desires of the flesh—the fruit of the spirit is love, joy, peace, patience, kindness, goodness, faithfulness, gentleness, self-control... If we live by the Spirit, let us also walk by the Spirit. Let us not become conceited provoking one another, envying one another.

"Love fuels healing, relationships, strength out of weakness, trust in faith, and hope...the ceaseless power of God's love and the moving force of love for positive change is eternal and more potent than the darkest of forces. It conquers revenge, fuels forgiveness, mends the broken, and tears down communication walls.

"The Gospel is an invitation to joy. The experience of communion with the Holy Trinity is profound joy. This joy isn't the superficial happiness we experience in our psychological highs and lows, but an unfathomable peace.

"Peace, well-being of body, mind, and soul. Peace connects our soul to the power, harmony, serenity, trust, hope, and solace in God's love and firm foundation. It infuses us with a peace that can endure changes in life, temporal pain that works to derail our faith, be it the death of a spouse, financial turmoil, or natural disaster. Living in the world, we cannot be immune to suffering, but the peace of God gives us the will to find joy in turmoil and search for opportunities to love during heartache. Most importantly, it gives us the security of eternal life in the spirit.

"Patience. With God's peace, we are equipped to bear the burden of suffering and sow love and faithfulness in times of unrest. The patience gives us perspective to grow in the gifts of the spirit.

"Generosity. The Holy Spirit is divine generosity of the Trinity. Filled with the spirit, we have the volition to give ourselves to the service of others. To carve a piece of we to uphold the weakest to greatest of life. This giving of us turns the ego upside down. We stop worrying about the selfish wants of our own existence, finding fulfillment in using our talents to serve others.

"Self-control—this is the hardest gift to accept. It is also a gift that we often try to manipulate. We think we can control our desire, only for it to come back fiercely and in dangerous power. We must see self-control as part of giving of ourselves. Realizing that the worldly desires we chase after cannot, nor will ever fulfill our needs. Only Christ can provide that sense of peace. So lay down your desire for revenge by exercising the self-control of forgiveness."

St. Michael's hosted a celebratory Pentecost picnic gathering in Jude Park. The potluck meal allowed the church community to break bread, sharing their portions in friendship and love. Dessert was a vanilla cake with red frosting from the Swan Valley Bakery.

"Your sermon moved me today," Susan said, catching up with Father Leo after church.

"How are things going?"

"I'm making progress. Step by step, I'm fighting to learn to forgive and let go of the fear and anger every day. The Bible study you organized for me has been a big help."

"Pray to the Holy Spirit for peace and discernment. Let the roots of faith and trust in God's care empower you in this process."

"I struggle, but I am turning my burdens over to Christ, seeking the spirit to guide me in this uncharted territory. I know that I'm not alone."

"I'm hearing wonderful things about your work at the lodge. You have devised a great lineup of activities."

"It has been a true joy."

"I received a note from my colleague in Bozeman about some of his parishioners, the Caseys. They are spending the last week of June at the Solitude Lake Lodge."

"I look forward to meeting them."

"The family is coping with the death of the fatherMark Casey. A pilot in Afghanistan, he died last year. He was gunned down, and his body was never recovered. The loss has devastated his widow, Teri, his sons, Chris and Max, and his daughter, Emma. It would be wonderful if you could reach out and ensure they have a warm welcome."

"Of course." Learning of the Caseys' plight was a stark reminder that she wasn't alone in grief. She could not use her misery as a banner, a mark of her identity. The broken must come together to heal, even if their sufferings are unique. You share the common bond of sorrow and the resiliency of hope.

Chapter 15

Rodeo, a symbol of the wild unbridled West. In rural Montana, rodeo ran far deeper than sport. It was a culture lassoing neighbors into a social atmosphere of excitement and fun.

The Hidden Creek Guest Ranch was located on the banks of Hidden Creek, five miles south of town. The ranch offered guests a chance to cowboy up on a small working cattle ranch, participating in the cattle drive, dredging sheep, learning how to ride and wrangle. They offered ranch immersion programs for all skill sets.

Stevie was the ranch's horse operations manager. She was a maestro who could ride, rope, tie, rustle, wrangle... She could do it all.

The Hidden Creek Ranch Rodeo featured entrants from across the state who competed for cash prizes, as well as resident wranglers to entertain the guests.

"Blancher." Stevie, fresh off her horse, came over to the stands to welcome her friend to the ruckus. "Thrilled that you could make it."

"This is my first rodeo in years."

"Hold your horses, it is going to be a doozy. The high school state champion bareback bull rider, Anson Aiken, is in the lineup today competing against old-time champion Ernst Earle. I'm heading the barrel racing. We have a good group of young cowgirls that I think are up for the challenge."

"I'd like to arrange a field trip for the Solitude Lake kids to the guest ranch for rope and tying. It would be a fun outing for them."

"The door's always open for you." Stevie nodded. "Where's Jake? Isn't he your date for the rodeo?"

"Jake and I are just friends."

"You don't sound too convinced." Stevie laughed, with a sly grin. "I know that you're recovering from Bradley's death and all the other junk he pulled, but don't use that as an excuse to ignore your feelings for Jake. You have a long history."

"History is what I'm afraid of."

"Don't be. Great guys only bow in from heaven once in a blue moon. You've got to lasso them in while the stars are dancing."

Jake had tossed and turned all night, unable to sleep as his mind fixated itself on Susan. He'd replayed last night's dance, the fire between them, frame by frame, scrutinizing every nanosecond. The warmth of her skin and scent of her hair lingered like dangling lilacs. Their chemistry was undeniable flare, fierce and passionate.

Every impulse told Jake to run into Susan's arms. Still, he hesitated. He longed for Susan's companionship like air to the lungs, but he could not risk the fallout of losing her again. He didn't want to risk the bare bones of their friendship falling apart as it was rebuilding muscle. He could destroy their relationship by confessing his secret love to Susan so soon after they'd rekindled the flame. For now, he would remain silent, the fire raging within him, hidden.

"I thought you'd stood me up," Susan teased before offering Jake a handful of her kettle corn.

"Miss the rodeo? Never."

"Glad to know you have your priorities straight." Susan tugged at his hand before stepping back. She had to control this spark before it burned too bright.

The call of the bugle and trumpet orchestra playing "The Star-Spangled Banner" signaled the start of the rodeo. Longtime emcee Rascal Everett announced the lineup, then rodeo clowns introduced the crowd to the junior barrel racers.

Barrel racing was a display of agility and skill on the part of both horse and rider. It was a race against the clock to maneuver a cloverleaf pattern around three barrels. Riders opted to start the pattern to the left or the right. The clock began when the horse and rider crossed the predetermined start line and stopped when they came back across the same line. Every fraction of a second counted, with tipped-over barrels adding five-second penalties to the time.

The first and second rider struggled, their horsesnwilling to cooperate as barrels tumbled. The third rider, a twelve-year-old standout, completed the course unscathed and in short time, winning the round.

A rope-tying entertainment comedy vignette with clowns served as a small break before the rough-hewn sport of bareback riding.

"This makes me nervous," Susan said, clamping her hand on Jake's knee.

"Nervous for the horse or rider?"

"Both," Susan admitted. She knew several high school friends who had been seriously injured in the "eight-second ride."

Bareback riding was one of the most physically demanding activities in the world of sports. A rider took a dangerous risk, sitting directly on a bucking horse, with only its "riggin" to hang on to. As the horse came out of the chute, the cowboy's feet had to be above the break of the horse's shoulders. He'd hold his feet up at least through the horse's first move, then spur the horse on each jump, matching the horse's rhythm and showing control rather than flopping around. He wasn't allowed to touch the horse, his equipment, or himself with his free hand. If the ride lasted eight seconds, two judges awarded up to twenty-five points for technique.

Five bareback riders dared to compete. In the end, Anson Aiken lived up to his state title, with power and grace he "danced" with steady agility atop the horse for nearly twelve seconds. Susan was just grateful that no one was injured.

Tie-down roping showcased the skills of preteen and teenage cowboys. The contest was a sprinting event in which the tie-down roper chased down the calf on horseback, throwing a loop over the calf's head. Then he'd step off the horse, tying the calf's three legs together with piggin' string.

The Sunday Rodeo ended with the granddaddy of all rodeo races, bull riding. The dangerous game had injured and killed its fair share of cowboys. Like the bareback riding competition, bull riders had to use strength and coordination to stay on the steer, riding its harsh and volatile movements.

"If I were the steer, I'd want to ram the rider," Susan expressed. "You can't blame the bull for being a bit temperamental. You can call the rider foolish."

"I suppose that foolish skill is the sheer excitement of the game."

With the dust settled in the corral, Susan and Jake began to say their goodnights.

"Interested in dinner? My treat?" Jake proposed.

"Hungry as I am, I have errands to run before heading back to the Lone Moose." It took extreme self-control not to fall into the invitation. "See you tomorrow at the lodge?"

"I'm counting down the seconds."

Chapter 16

The month of June moved at lightning pace. Long sun-drenched days coupled with dazzling star-dusted nights propelled Susan to a cautious confidence and apprehensive joy.

The peace of the lake stirred the spirit within her to break free from the anger and bitterness that had defined her the past six months. The process to reclaim her sense of self in the avalanche of tragedy was invigorated by her work at the lodge.

Susan fell into the rhythm of the season, allowing herself to enjoy the simple pleasure of wading in the water, dancing in the summer breeze, playing hide-and-seek with five-year-olds.

Witnessing the constant sense of discovery in the eyes and hearts of children, Susan was spurred to dig in the dirt, not concerned with the grime, but content in the joy of uncovering lessons in buried trash and treasure. Suddenly the blazing stars weren't tears in the night, each cluster of fire a story beckoning her to rediscover what she thought was life. The spark breaking the deep abyss.

Was Susan completely healed? No. But she was making steps, crossing the bridge of recovery. With each step she cut herself on jagged sharp memories, wrestling with ghosts and exorcising the haunted layers one by one. With each painful blow, the agony of loss lessened slightly. It was a silent conflict, juxtaposed by competing paradoxes, as the sweet halcyon of her past ruptured angrily into the present tense.

"How do you reconcile two faces, two sides as one coin?" Susan debated. "How do I reconcile the pure-hearted person I fell in love with so long ago with the callous stranger revealed in death. Was the life I knew before ever real, or just a shadow?"

At some intersection, Bradley had fractured. He'd defiled himself.

He became broken and, in the process, injured those who loved him. Susan reminded herself constantly that it wasn't her burden to reconcile the two faces of Bradley Dixon. His flesh was dead, and his soul left to God. Only his divine generosity could mend the brokenness.

Susan made a point to carve out space in the quiet solace of early morning to contemplate the gray area of life. It was in the bridge of light and dark, with the sun rising over the grip of night, that raw heavy emotions trickled in. It was then that she wrestled with phantoms, exorcising the fear and hate layer by layer.

The point of Susan's contention, dangling like an elephant on a tightrope, was her attraction to Jake. It would be a lie to claim that this rekindling fire was unexpected. The roots of their relationship, fierce and strong, had been planted in infancy. The foundation of their love started as friendship, a friendship able to weather the elements of change and upheaval against the chaos in the world. Sometimes the deepest friendships straddled the boundaries of love and duty. Susan and Bradley had fallen in love with one another when they were teenagers, neither one wanting to risk losing the security of friendship. They buried the passion, refusing to confront the boundaries of love and friendship. In the end, they'd surrendered the fight, each divided, separate and alone.

Bradley had been Susan's true love, but he wasn't her first love. That distinction belonged to Jake Arnett.

Susan suspected Jake had loved her once and his "friends only" mantra was a defense mechanism to prevent a fracture in their relationship. When a teenage Susan confronted Jake about his feelings, he shied away. Bradley fought hard to win Susan's heart. In the end, she relented. She closed her regret, accepting that her love for Jake was destined to be a ghost.

I can't regret the past, but I do wonder "what if" I'd married Jake instead of Bradley, Susan mulled in the silence of her heart.

"Susan?" A petite attractive brunette in her mid-forties approached. "I'm Teri Casey."

"Welcome to Solitude. Father Leo mentioned your visit." Susan was emanating warmth.

"We are thrilled to be here. My twin sons, Chris and Max, along with my teenage daughter, Emma, look forward to participating in the Solitude Explorers program."

"The week ahead is jam-packed with excitement—hiking, kayaking, games, camping, a naturalist talk about Lewis and Clark…oh, and tonight a campfire folklore lecture about Blackfeet legends."

"My husband, Mark, died fifteen months ago." Teri's tone was heavy. "My kids are still struggling, particularly Emma…"

"I'm struggling with the loss of my husband as well." Susan comforted Teri. "Grief affects everyone in different ways. The notes might vary but the tune is a symphony we all relate too. I do believe that Solitude Lake has the power to heal."

"I hope so." Teri bit her lip, mulling her thoughts, her tilted brows revealing conflict. "I took a leap, inviting a family friend, Tom Murphy, to accompany us. The boys are delighted to have Tom along to take them fishing, but Emma is furious… I don't know how to get through to her. If only I can make her understand…"

"There are many levels of understanding. I don't know the emotions your daughter is facing. I know her reality is harsh. You're both suffering a loss. It takes time and patience to heal, and even then, I'm not sure you ever fully forget the heartache.

It's a scar that fades. I'm not one to give advice—I'm searching for answers myself. I do know that you both need each other right now. It's easy to put up walls and to be angry, but deep down your daughter loves you. Talk to her. Be honest with one another."

"I try talking to her, but she keeps pushing me away. She blames me for moving on. I have moved on to a point. As a parent you don't have the luxury of hiding in a room, crying your heart out. I put up a strong front for my children. It doesn't mean that I'm not hurting."

"Tell your daughter what you told me," Susan encouraged. "If she doesn't listen the first time, then be patient with her. Give her time and space, all the while reinforcing your love for her and the love that you had for your husband."

"It's just complicated."

"Your 'friendship' with Tom Murphy?" Susan guessed.

"I'm between a rock and a hard place. I don't want to mope around agonizing and rehashing my husband's death, but when it comes to embracing love, even tinkering with the idea again, it feels like a betrayal. I know that Bob would want me to be happy. Tom makes me happy, and he loves the kids as his own. Emma thinks I'm a heartless witch because I'm dating again. She accuses me of spitting on her father's grave because I'm going out with his best friend. Frankly, I'm at my wit's end."

"Love heals all wounds—the fear is rushing blindly, retreating into an ill-fated rebound that only adds confusion to a tattered soul. At the same time, do you risk losing a chance at love due to the threat of another broken heart? I don't have that answer. I'm torn with moving on. At times I'm guilty of finding happiness in the sunset or calm in the rain. Voices screaming, 'Your husband is dead,' 'You should be angry or miserable.' I know how hard it is to trust again, especially in love. It is a complex situation and one that you must navigate yourself. Search for a balance. Realize the collision of mourning and joy is a tangled road, but you and Emma owe it to yourselves to try to walk beside one another in this process, even if your paces differ."

"I apologize for baring my soul. I'm usually more thick-skinned." Teri's flushed face was covered in tears.

"Tom sounds like a good catch. I know you don't want to hurt him, or your kids. Take things slow and be honest. Tell Emma that just because you have feelings for another man, it doesn't lessen the love you have for her father. Take time to talk about your husband as a family. The good times and how you fell in love… Don't see his death as a shadow, but as a light. I know he's looking down on you and the kids. He wants you to be happy."

"You are an angel. Thank you for listening."

"I'm just a fractured soul, searching for understanding just like you." Susan smiled. "We're having an ice-cream party in the lodge later tonight, followed by a stargazing party. The forecast calls for northern lights. Nothing soothes the mind like Moose Tracks and a star-filled wilderness sky."

The wind rustled against the trees as the chill of night sent a shiver down Susan's spine. Nighttime temperatures in the Rockies shifted dramatically as the fiery sun descended behind the mountains, eighty-degree temps sharply dropping to the mid-forties.

Susan sat on the docks, the half-moon reflecting in the water as the Milky Way and thousands of stars scattered across the night. She savored the last bite of ice cream before pulling on her fleece sweatshirt.

She sat there, lost in the wind.

"'I never tire of the night, to see such bright stars in the sky. The stories in the galaxies, yes we exist so fragile a fire, the silent rift…'" Jake's voice broke the silence.

"That's the poem I wrote senior year." Susan said, surprised he remembered it.

"I have a copy in my bedside drawer." Jake looked deep into Susan's stormy green eyes. "Do you still write?"

"No, time got in the way. Other priorities, I suppose. I have my old poetry notebook buried deep in the closet."

"You should dig it out. Start composing again."

"The ink in my pen dried up a long time ago."

"You're in luck. I have pen full of ink ready for paper. I listen to you as you engineer your folktales around the campfire. The kids are rapt in the quick wit and adventure. You should write your folktales about Solitude in a book."

"For the record, those are my great-grandfather's stories." Susan dismissed her creative acumen, changing the subject. "Do you think we'll see the northern lights?"

"Time will tell." Jake remembered the summer of their junior year, the northern lights dancing above the water with such intense fire. It was then that he began to recognize his love for Susan was deeper than friendship. He had nearly kissed her that night, but Bradley—the new kid in town—sat down on the docks, striking up conversation.

Two weeks later Susan's father died. The timing didn't seem right for Jake to admit his feelings that summer. While Bradley, rebelling against his father, connected with Susan on a level that sparked jealousy. Jake held close to that jealousy, anger, and fear driving him to resentment. It seemed foolish now.

"The northern lights are collisions between gaseous particles in the earth's atmosphere with charged particles released from the sun's atmosphere. I find it comforting that such disorder can create a still beauty—a spectacular eruption of color. Even in crisis there is a fierce peace." Jake clutching Susan's hand.

They remained quiet for the better part of ten minutes, both afraid to speak what they dreamed of saying.

"Dad used to tell me that the northern lights were the lonely hearts that had died, releasing their sorrow and dancing in joy as they met their maker on the other side. It seems fitting that an explosion of light is the collision of intense suffering, with abounding joy. You struggle at first with that overpowering love, then succumb to its healing force with courage, hope, and yearning. This place, Solitude Lake, it has made my heart dance again. I'm still cluttered...but there is a joy in my spirit."

"Your dad always said that Solitude Lake has mystical healing powers." Jake stalled. "This summer has changed me. I'm learning to let go too."

"Of what?"

"Regret, anger, jealousy..."

Susan almost broached the unsettling topic of their past, before letting it disappear with the wind.

"Aurora borealis means 'dawn of the north.' Let's toast to the new dawn."

Just then the raging colors of the northern lights burst out of the sky, dancing against the mountains, reflecting in the healing waters of Solitude Lake.

Chapter 17

"I'll be honest. I don't want to be here." Emma Casey's cheeks were fiery red as she slammed her foot down. "I'm seventeen years old, soon to enter my senior year at Bozeman High School—the idea of running around playing pin the tail on the donkey and kids' camp games is not my idea of a vacation."

"Participation in the program is voluntary," Susan said, hoping to connect with Emma. "There are lots of teenage Explorers that you can connect with. This week's itinerary includes kayaking, hiking, a movie night, a cookout, and a back country camping trip. Or we have options like arts and crafts, bird-watching, photography…"

"I don't want to connect with anyone. I want to be alone, solitude, get it? I didn't want to come on this stupid trip. I'd rather be back at home, hanging with my friends. Instead, I'm stuck in the middle of nowhere with nothing to do."

"There's plenty to do if you open up your mind to a little fun. I know that given the circumstances it's easy to sit around and sulk. I've been there recently. I guarantee you that this week will go by much faster if you take time to have fun."

"My dad is dead; my mom is a tyrant who's letting that angler Tom reel her in. Nothing about my life is fun. It's a horrible existence," Emma said, flashing the "me against the world" attitude teenagers often clung to. Susan could sympathize with Emma's pity-party. She could not count the times she'd sat on a ledge and felt sorry for herself.

"Get your hiking boots on," Susan demanded.

"Don't boss me around." Emma feigned defiance.

"You can go on a hike with me, right now, or you can go fishing with Tom and your brothers, moping in your misery."

"I was going to stay in the cabin," Emma argued.

"All I'm asking for is one hour. At the end of that hour, if you want to go and hide in the cabin, lashing out at the world, fine."

"One hour." Emma begrudgingly caved in.

While Emma changed, Susan radioed junior counselor Candace Cafferty. Candace was a peppy twenty-two-year-old who put in fifteen hours a week at the lodge assisting with arts and recreation. Candace agreed to engage the rest of the Explorers in an art project for the next hour.

"Let's go," Susan directed, leading the teen down the dusty gravel spur road that connected to the Solitude trail system.

"Where is everyone else?" Emma trudged along.

"Your peers are in the Lewis Center, working on an arts and crafts project and watching a documentary about Glacier National Park."

"Hate to miss that action," she said, her tone sarcastic. "Why are you ditching the group to force me on a hike?"

Susan didn't immediately offer a reply.

"Did you bring your camera?"

"Who needs pictures? I want to forget this trip as soon as possible, not revel in bad memories."

"I have my digital camera, just in case." Susan remained upbeat. "We're going to hike to a special spot, Storm Point."

"Yeah, whatever." Emma shrugged.

For the next two miles, no words were exchanged between them. Susan wanted to give Emma time to collect her thoughts and be stirred by the scenery. The trail zigzagged through the woods, going up steep inclines before easing into an alpine meadow scattered with colorful wildflowers. Two months ago, Susan would have trudged through this trail much like Emma, counting down seconds, made anxious and weary by unfair circumstances.

As her feet trampled lightly over the well-beaten path, her senses filled with the complex web of life. The camouflaged butterfly leapt out, while the purple flowers contrasted with the arid brush. Susan could only hope that for a minute Emma might uncover a new layer in her wilderness, the diversity of trees brimming with life and hope instead of the dead stump she perched upon.

"How much farther?" Emma pestered, looking at her watch. Susan ignored the question, instead offering her a sip of water.

"You used to go hiking with your dad a lot."

"What is it to you?"

"I hiked Hyalite Canyon's Palisade Falls trail when I was at MSU for a seminar several summers ago. Did you and your dad have a special hike, a local trail haunt you'd escape to on the weekends?"

"Did my mom put you up to this?" Emma rolled her eyes into the back of her head with a heavy stammer.

"She cares about you."

"If she cared about my brothers and me, she wouldn't be getting engaged to Tom Murphy."

"You didn't answer my question." Susan knew that Emma needed to release her frustration. "Tell me about the hiking adventures with your dad? A favorite memory."

"Like you care."

"Try me."

"Fairy Lake. My dad and I hiked to Fairy Lake in the Gallatin National Forest north of Bozeman in the Bridger Canyon a few weeks before he was deployed. He wasn't supposed to go back to Afghanistan. He was a doctor, not a soldier. He joined the military reserves to help pay for college. It was his seventh deployment. He always said, 'Lucky seven.' Bullshit, really," Emma tried to hide her tears. "Fairy Lake—

if there's magic in this world, you can find it there with the towering snowcapped Bridger Range lifting up to the sky, the clouds so close you can nearly touch them…the steep jagged cliffs, so scrambled and yet so beautiful. It isn't easy to get to Fairy Lake. You can hike in over the 'M' Trail, across Sacajawea Peak then down to the base of the lake or drive in tumbling over a gravel road that I'm not sure is a real road at all. It has giant rocks that can flatten tires if you're not careful and hundreds of free ranging cattle that will run you off the road."

"A true adventure."

"Dad usually packed all us kids into his Jeep. Mom isn't much on camping. This time was different—just me and Dad. It was the thick of July and it was hot and the ground was dry. We survived the rocky road to Fairy Lake and set up our tent at dusk. The cool part is we were the only people at the campsite. Dad ignited the fire while I made sandwiches. After dinner we roasted marshmallows and gazed at the stars. He said, 'I'm not good with astronomy, but I know where to find the North Star. Polaris guides us home and reminds us that though we are far apart, we can see that same star, in this hemisphere and the next…' I think he knew, instinct or psychic intuition, that he wasn't coming back home. We woke up at sunrise. We just sat there for hours and talked. We finished the day hiking around the edge of the lake. I wish I could go back to that moment right now."

"The story about Polaris, my dad often spoke the same words," Susan remembered fondly. "Take it as a gift. Know that your dad loved you and he's with you in spirit. Look at the North Star and know that you aren't alone."

Silence passed between the pair until they reached Storm Point. The dramatic cliff just out of the forest offered stunning views of Solitude Lake and the mountains. They sat down on a nearby bench, taking in the views.

"Why is this called Storm Point?" Emma inquired, unable to imagine squalls in the serenity of the spot.

"There's a legend passed down in my family that explains the etymology of this spot. There was once a young girl, radiant and beautiful. The Great Spirit gave her the power to control the weather. One day she encountered a hunter on the ridge. She cried out to him not to shoot the doe, for she knew it had a fawn hiding in the woods, hungry and alone. The hunter and the girl fell in love. She was engaged to another, not out of love but because her father struck a peace deal with a neighboring tribe. When he learned that his daughter was secretly seeing the hunter, he admonished her. She promised that for peace in the area with the neighboring tribe, she would marry the chief's son, but begged for one last chance to see the hunter. Her father agreed. The girl and the hunter met at Storm Point. She explained the situation and he agreed to let her go. He asked that she use the dew to draw up the 'wilder flower,' every year at this spot so that he could remember their love. Her tears drew up the flowers. As they began to kiss one last time, the girl's father, seeing the hunter as a threat, shot him in the back with his bow and arrow. The hunter died instantly, falling off the cliff into the lake, where he is said to protect swimmers from drowning. The girl cried out in anger, storm clouds turning the sky black. Lightning struck the cliff with such force an earthquake could be felt for miles. The final bolt struck her in the heart—she too perished."

"What a sad story... How could her father kill her beloved?"

"He realized his mistake instantly and cried out to the Creator for forgiveness. The storms continued to erupt from this rock every day after she died. The man, disconsolate, did not leave the spot, praying that his daughter and her lover were in the hands of God, while dealing with his anger. Now, the man was a great leader to his people, and they yearned for him to return to them. They feared with his daughter dead, the peace treaty would be null and void and their enemies would force them into a bloody battle. On the anniversary of her death, the father was about to jump off a ledge, when the wilder flower came up from the ground. He saw a vision of his daughter and her lover rise from the lake below.

"'Father, I was angered by your hate; it burned so deep that the fire of hope nearly burned out. Yet in death I was raised to the heavens. My peace is pure, and I am reconciled with my lover. Your heart is heavy because you hate yourself. You have repented; go forward with the blessing of life and redeem yourself before our people. There is a great battle coming over the hill. Hundreds will be slaughtered if you do not lead them to safety. Take the wilder berry and make a drink, strong and bitter. It will give you the strength of the Great Spirit to be healed and to rescue those in peril.'

"Suddenly, visions of war and how to avert it came into the man's mind like wildfire. He did precisely as his daughter told him. Strong with the wilder berry, he saved his people from the enemy. In time a peace treaty that lasted for eternity was reached. Peace is on this land. Yet storms still strike, trying to lead us off a cliff. Remember the forgiveness and peace of the girl and her lover."

"Why did she forgive her father?"

"What do you think?"

"I suppose that we all make stupid decisions. She should have been able to marry the hunter. Yet she gave up that chance for happiness to please her father. Even then he killed the hunter and she died in grief. It created chaos in the heart of her father, and his people suffered. He learned that he was at fault, and I think she realized that although his actions were horrible, we are flawed and he deserved a second chance, so that he could sacrifice to save his people instead of allowing his grief and anger to block those in his care from receiving leadership in battle. In turn he saved others, because of her forgiveness and love. His love for his daughter made him realize the error of his ways."

"My dad and I used to hike together too. This was our favorite hiking spot. He died when I was around your age. I was at this spot with Jake Arnett, an operations manager at the lodge, when my future husband, Bradley Dixon, ran screaming through the woods, 'There's been an emergency…Susan— your father had a heart attack. He's dead. I'm sorry.' At that moment I wanted to jump off that cliff, fall into the lake, and drown in my sorrows."

"But you didn't?"

"No. In the agony of the moment, I saw a bushel of wilder berry. I remembered his love. I felt his spirit engulf me in love and peace. I knew that this storm would be fierce, but the lake would heal me. I knew that he wanted me to live and to love. It took me a while to understand that we don't betray those we've lost by moving on. We still carry their light within us. The problem is if we don't live and love, their light is a convoluted shadow of misery, pain, and anger. The storms won't pass."

"That's how I feel right now," Emma admitted.

"To tell you the truth, I still feel that way from time to time. My husband, Bradley, died in a freak car accident in December. It isn't easy, moving on. Frankly, I don't like that expression, 'moving on.' You never really move on from love, you rest in it. A true love stays with you. Really moving on is about discovering new hope and detaching yourself from the web of guilt, bitterness, and anger. You rest in the spirit of love. It's a much happier place."

"I'm sorry about your husband."

"I wish I had the power to bring your dad back. I do trust that he's in heaven, where peace is eternal."

"It's not that I don't like Tom. He's always been there for our family. I don't even mind my mom marrying him…it just feels too quick, too abrupt. Why isn't she still grieving?"

"Trust me, your mom is grieving. She's struggling with embracing her feelings for Tom, trying to reconcile the fact she feels as though she's betraying your father. She worries about you. She told me that she would sacrifice her happiness if it made you feel secure and safe. If you don't like Tom, then she won't marry him. If Tom were a bad guy, then yeah, you should protest their relationship, but Tom seems like a stand-up gentleman. He loves your mom, and she loves him. It isn't the same sort of love she had for your dad. Trust me, I will always love Bradley, but I do think it's okay to love again."

"It's just so soon."

"Talk to her. Tell her how you feel, but don't be selfish. Intuition tells me that fear is driving you to push Tom away. Deep down you really care about him, almost as much as your dad. You're afraid that if you start to rely on him as a stepdad, it would mean betraying your dad. You also cling to the loss and grief, because it's such a real and raw emotion…it almost connects you to your father, but it's unhealthy. Find memories of your dad in joy, not in fear. It might take time to warm up to Tom but give him a chance. Most importantly, talk to your mom. You need each other, more than you realize."

"I have been selfish Not on purpose… I guess I'm afraid. Things are changing so fast. I'm afraid that I'll forget…"

"Look to the North Star. Polaris. You won't forget."

Emma and Susan bonded over the next week. It was an unlikely friendship, yet circumstances threw them together. Emma became an active participant in the Solitude Explorers program while she started to make inroads with her mother. And she even enjoyed a fishing trip with Tom.

Chapter 18

Return to sender. The bloodred stamp posted across the certified letter she had sent to Ellis Dixon weeks before was stuffed in her post office box. *Angry* was the short word to describe her annoyance with his blatant disregard of letters discussing the burial of his son.

While in town, Susan picked up Fourth of July supplies, from party food to decorations, a flag, and printouts for her camp arts and crafts project. She swung by the church to pick up the book Father Leo had ordered for her to accompany the September seminar. *The Beautiful Letdown: Finding God's Light in Despair.*

Fourth of July in Hidden Creek was small-town Americana at its best, with a distinct Western edge. With three lakes within sight of the town's city limits, water recreation was at the heart of the festivities. A flotilla on Mystic Lake started the day with a parade of red, white, and blue...the small yet mighty marching band of Hidden Creek on the barge playing Sousa and George Cohan. The boat parade decorations ranged from "Uncle SamAmerica Boat," to a Bob Marshall Wilderness–inspired float, as well as creative dragon boats.

The float parade was followed by the Bite of Hidden Creek, where local vendors and farmers sampled their best treats. The hotly contested pie contest put the grand dames of baking against one another.

As the sun went down, the town migrated to Solitude Lake to watch the fireworks boomerang over the water. A BBQ and dance were held at the lodge, with proceeds going to local charities.

Susan looked forward to the Fourth of July–themed activities leading up to the fireworks. She hoped that the campers would enjoy the Fourth of July pre-day festivities, such as Red, White, and Blue Tag Team, a screening of the film *1776*, an art contest, decorating patriotic cookies, water balloons, and much more

The Arnett brothers spared no expense in the Solitude Lake Lodge float. The theme: American Glory. Jake had been tight-lipped about the float's appearance, only saying that it would "make the founders proud."

"Think you have enough shopping bags?" Jake assisted Susan in unloading her car by the Lewis Center.

"You can never go overboard with Fourth of July fun. It's going to be a patriotic couple of days," Susan said, upbeat. "And for the record, half of these decorations are for Keeley. She's adorning the barn in red, white, and blue for the dance." The word *dance* triggering a flicker of tension as Jake and Susan both thought about their last dance.

"Are you going to the dance?" Jake mustered.

"It would be unpatriotic not to. I just have to decide what I'm going to wear."

"You look great in anything, Blancher." Jake touched her shoulder. Her skin was warm from the sunlight. "Save me a dance."

"The first and the last."

The smell of cupcakes fresh out of the oven was enough to spur kids and adults into a frenzy.

"They have to cool first. Then we can decorate them," Susan told her campers as they reached for the cake.

"Who cares about decorating—when can we eat them?" a spunky seven-year-old questioned.

"The icing is the best part," a pretty redhead with a handmade ruffled flag-patterned dress contested.

"Patience is a virtue. After we make our pinwheels, we'll decorate our cupcakes."

"Then can we eat?"

"Yes, then we can eat." Susan laughed.

The festive mood at the lodge was contagious. Everyone buzzed with excitement as the holiday activities neared. On her lunch break Susan assisted Keeley with hanging decorations in the barn.

"You're doing an amazing job," Keeley complimented.

"It's easy to work when you have this much fun."

"You and Jake have really reconnected."

"Time can't put a wedge between best friends." Susan shrugged, downplaying the relationship.

"Jake loves you. That may not be the politically correct thing to say, but it is the truth."

"He made it clear years ago that love was not on his mind, at least not with me. We're just friends."

"Are you really that clueless? Jake has always loved you. He just got scared. He didn't want to mess up your friendship. In the end, he wound up with a broken heart. He's stubbornly worn it on his sleeve for years"

"I better get back to the campers." Susan feigned an excuse to end the conversation.

"I know that you're afraid," Keeley said, not letting Susan off the hook.

"Afraid?"

"Of admitting that you love Jake. Fear of letting go of Bradley…"

Susan, her face flushed, left the conversation, irritated at Keeley. She claimed to be irritated by the preposterous assumption that she was in love with Jake… In truth, she was irritated because Keeley had her emotions pegged to a T.

Waking up with a headache, Susan downed an aspirin. The sunrise, full of fire red, hearkened Independence Day with a brash glow.

How had things gotten so convoluted in the space of twenty-four hours? She'd stayed up the better part of the wee hours of the morning, her thoughts wrapped up in thoughts of Jake Arnett and feelings of guilt.

Why did she feel as if she were betraying Bradley for being attracted to Jake? The husband she knew would have been the first in line, at least in death, to lay down his jealous contention and encourage a romance with Jake Arnett. The darker side of Bradley had turned her world upside down and allowed her to fall flat on her face, without so much as a warning or courtesy of an explanation. Susan had searched through the paperwork in Seattle, hoping to find a note of some kind explaining the treachery he left behind. Nothing.

I know logically I shouldn't fall into a rebound romance, but is it really a rebound if I've always loved Jake?"

Susan cleared her head with a shower before getting ready for the flotilla. She buried the debate in the shadows, for the sake of enjoying the holiday.

Mystic Lake was the largest of the tri-lakes in Hidden Creek. It was named for the myth that beneath its waters was a gateway to another world. As a child, the story had fascinated Susan, though she realized that it was meant to make sense of those who drowned by the strange vortex funnel from a nearby cave.

Susan, accompanied by Beth and Glen, set her blanket down on a patch of sand on the Point Royale day-use area, amidst the more than one thousand spectators.

"It never ceases to amaze the level of creativity and hard work forged to bring these floats to life," Beth enthused as a bugle signaled the start of the flotilla.

"I'm eager to see the Solitude Lake Lodge float. The Arnett Boys have tiptoed around, working in total secrecy the past few weeks, bringing their inspiration to life. They have their heart set on winning the grand prize."

The first boat to drift down the promenade was the Marmot Books float. Designed with a storybook theme, characters such as Hansel and

Gretel, Bilbo Baggins, Cinderella, and Johnny Appleseed brought the concept to life.

The Timber's Edge went with a 1950s theme, with the staff in poodle skirts and leather jackets, dancing to the beats of Elvis.

The Hidden Creek Ranger Station helmed a National Forest theme with Smokey the Bear, "Only you can prevent forest fires."

"It's the Solitude Lake Lodge float," Susan cheered. "*Washington Crossing the Delaware*. Gilligan is playing Washington."

"Gilligan leading an army. God help us," Glen joked.

"I for one am impressed." Beth shouted her support. "The Arnett boys outdid themselves."

The last of the floats harbored in the Mystic Marina, just after eleven o'clock. The crowds dispersed, transitioning to downtown Hidden Creek for food heaven at "The Bite."

Front and Belton Streets, lined with over forty food vendors in a culinary feast ranging from Montana beef skewers to Flathead pulled pork, Asian fusion, Mexican, Italian, salmon cakes, cotton candy, kettle corn, potato tornados, hand-churned ice cream, hotdogs, corn on the cob, fried dough, a beer and wine tent, pie contest, and much more.

"To heck with my diet today," Beth said, intent on indulging in the fair food.

"Jake convinced me to go on a ten-mile hike tomorrow to Holland Point, so a celebratory break in calorie counting is justified."

"Let's toast to Independence Day." Glen raised up his IPA.

The Bite was a huge block party that brought the vibrant community together. It was an opportunity to catch up with friends and neighbors over huckleberry lemonade and Flathead cherry pie. Scoops were divulged and summer plans discussed. You wouldn't find a sweeter spot on Fourth of July in small-town America.

Full after going whole-hog, dabbling in a savory assortment of treats, Susan meandered down to Belton City Park, where the Marching Band was in full regalia trumpeting up American patriotic standards as city officials prepared to announce winners for the parade and pie contests.

She searched the crowd for Jake, instead running into Molly and Gilligan.

"Congrats on the tremendous float. You were a great General George, Gill."

"I'm just glad we didn't sink the boat."

"If you're looking for Jake, he's not here." Molly's tone was brusque. "He's helping Keeley with the finishing touches on tonight's big soiree at the lodge."

"Are you coming to the dance and fireworks extravaganza?" Gilligan turned to Susan.

"I wouldn't miss it."

"Mayor Crowfoot is about to announce the contest winners."

Jim Crowfoot, a Blackfoot American, had served as Hidden Creek mayor for eight years. He had a strong focus on community, jobs, tourism, and conservation. His laid-back, focused personality makes him a popular neighbor and leader.

"It was a difficult decision for our sweet-toothed pie panel, helmed by our resident pie lady, Maeve Benson. After many succulent bites of pie, we have a winner. The award for Hidden Creek's Best Pie goes to Winnie Riggins, for her delicious marionberry streusel pie. She wins a $250 gift certificate to

Swan Valley Grocers, along with a gift basket of goodies from downtown retailers," Jim announced. "I know that our parade participants and spectators have been waiting in anxious anticipation for the Float your Boat Fourth Awards. This was no easy contest. I'll turn over the microphone to flotilla coordinator, Mystic Marina manager, Paul Bartlett."

"Our committee of twelve members from the community, ranging in backgrounds, viewed the boats just prior to and during the flotilla. We applaud the efforts of entrants for their hard work and creativity. In truth, all deserve a prize. However, there can only be one grand prize winner. That honor goes to…The Dragon's Flare Boat, constructed by the Cancer Support Community of Hidden Creek. You receive $1,000 and this majestic trophy, courtesy of Mystic Outfitters."

"At least we lost to a good cause. Cancer Support contributes so much to those dealing with cancer." Gilligan smiled in defeat.

"Our second-place winner, the creativity of storytelling brought alive, the Marmot Books float. You receive a $250 prize."

"That's brilliant," Nick and Lacy reveled. "We plan to donate the cash prize to the food bank."

"And finally, the runner-up, third-place winners, those daring Arnett Boys of Solitude Lake who crossed the Delaware with George 'Gilligan' Washington with patriotic glory. You receive a $100 gift certificate to the Hidden Creek General Store."

"Job well done." Molly tipped her hat, proud of her sons' accomplishment.

"The true prize was working on the float—we had a blast," Gil said, excited. "I can't complain about winning third place. Jake and Russ will be happier than a cowboy at the rodeo."

"We better get back to the lodge." Molly took notice of the time. "There's still a lot of work to do before tonight's fireworks display and barn dance."

"Save me a dance, Blancher—Jake doesn't get to dance will you all night," Gill teased.

"Goodbye, Susan." Molly's voice was cold. She remained ambivalent regarding Jake and Susan's burgeoning relationship. Her son had not been happier in years, yet she continued to fear that Susan's broken past would prevent their romance from taking a firm root. It was dangerous territory in her mind. "I pray that the only sparks flying tonight are the Independence Day fireworks."

Chapter 19

The crackle of light, exploding against the night, startled, banging and popping as the lake reflected colors of red, white, and blue.

Susan sat on the dock, her thoughts lost, submerged in past summers, each erupting firework blasting down a wall of memories she'd buried deep. She'd sat with Bradley on the shores of Solitude Lake the year before. He had whispered in her ear, "I love you," with a sweet kiss on her cheek.

Her anger burst with the intensity of the fireworks. Love and hurt. Betrayal and misunderstanding. Why had Bradley pursued her love? Was she his project, a broken fragile creature he wanted to mend, only to control and manipulate? Was his love motivated by his desire to avenge his father's abuse? He had made a point of throwing their relationship in his father's face, salt in a wound, every chance he got. Or was it just love?

The bitter sulfur scent, a brief reminder of a night long ago when she sat, bare feet off the dock, watching the flames, spectacular fire burning before dissipating, smote by the water below. The first Fourth of July after her dad's death. Susan was seventeen, alone, and Bradley had comforted her, drying her tears. That was when their friendship became muddy.

Susan was tugged in different directions by boys who were becoming men.

Now, Susan wanted desperately to fall heavy into Jake's arms.

"You look as if you have the mysteries of the universe on your mind?" Jake lightly tapped Susan on her shoulder.

"Thoughts run deep. Right now, I'm just enjoying the view. The fireworks are spectacular."

"You discovered the sweet spot," Jake noted.

Silence, as the grand finale awed with a barrage of sizzling lights. In an instant the fireworks stopped, and abruptly the night sky became a dark, smoky cloud, the remnants of the explosive power exposed.

"The dance is starting soon." Susan noted the time.

"First and last dance, right?" Jake leaned in with a whisper.

Without words, the pair, armed by the moonlight, trampled through the darkness to the barn dance. The luster of lantern light beckoned Jake and Susan inside the barn. The strings of the fiddle, pluck of the banjo, and strumming of guitar started the dance with a light swing-romp.

Susan and Jake stepped out onto the floor, their heels clacking as they rendezvoused in rhythm. One dance turned into three. Time at a near standstill.

During the first intermission, the lodge catering crew served a giant tart cake in an American flag design with fresh blueberries, raspberries, strawberries, and sweet cream frosting. It was served alongside hand-squeezed lemonade and patriotic punch.

The pair separated for half an hour as friends approached with hearty conversation.

"You and Jake are on fire," Harley Ethlers said, gracefully blunt as always. "Call me crazy, but it looks like you're tangled up in romance?"

"You are crazy." Susan hid behind the veil of laughter.

"You always were keen on each other. I was shocked when I found out that you'd ran off and married Bradley Dixon."

"Life is complicated."

"It doesn't have to be. Don't be afraid of falling when there's someone to catch you on the other end of the line."

"I need to get my oil changed next week. I'll be in touch." Susan's attempt at shifting the conversation was a thin mask.

Jake and Susan reconnected towards the end of the dance, like moths to the flame, magnetic.

"You look ravishing." Jake softly whispered in Susan's ear.

"Don't make me blush," Susan said, retreating into Jake's green eyes.

The music transitioned from a rambling swing into a slow waltz.

"It is getting late. I probably should get some sleep," Susan breathed. "We have a date tomorrow."

"A date?" Jake's half grin reeled her in. "Dates are romantic affairs."

"A ten-mile date with a hiking trail," Susan teased. "Then again, my dad always used to say hiking is a romantic ascent into the clouds."

"I think you should stay a little longer, just one more dance."

"Don't blame me if my feet tire halfway up the mountain."

"I'll carry you to the summit."

"Don't be ridiculous."

"There's nothing that I wouldn't do for you," Jake said honestly.

The two gave up the fight, drawn into a flawless kiss. No words were spoken after the embrace. No regrets, not tonight.

The slow original ballad switched to the Bob Wills dance classic, Stay a little longer.
"""

"I'll dance with you all night," Jake whispered in Susan's ear.

Dance they did. Until the barn lights flickered out.

Chapter 20

Jake dragged the covers over his head as the sun blistered through cracks in the blinds. Susan's caress haunted his senses like a wild dream he didn't want to wake up from. He tightly clutched the bottled lightning of their kiss, holding it in his heart like fireflies dancing in a mason jar.

The couple parted on the cusp of midnight under the fullness of the moon. The solitary confinement of their hearts ruptured, shattering silence like fireworks bursting out of the mountains. The pounding desire of their hearts danced in the desperate hope of love, guarded and unhinged.

On the other side of the lake, Susan awoke from her first full night's sleep since Bradley died. A rising calm crashed down her barricades of fear, igniting a ceasefire within. Joy burst at the seams, giddy and feverish, as it cautiously tested the water.

"I had a wonderful time with you at the dance." Susan searched for words as she climbed into Jake's truck for their expedition to Echo Canyon.

"The memory is forever etched in my mind. *Perfect* doesn't come close to describing the magic of last night." They breathed in the heat of the summer air as they wound through the Old Logger Road to the Echo Canyon trailhead.

"This is my first time hiking Echo Canyon," Susan commented.

"Prepare to be numbed by awe-inspiring beauty at every turn."

"I'm ready to explore the great unknown." Susan put her hand on Jake's knee.

Before hitting the trail, the pair feasted on a picnic lunch of ham-and-cheese sandwiches in the pine shade of the Echo Creek day-use area.

Echo Canyon was one of the most daunting and tantalizing hikes in the Hidden Creek area. The trail started off by meandering along the banks of Echo Creek through riparian flora and open-forest topography. The trail gradually gained elevation dancing through wildflower leas and muddy stretches of snowmelt, crisscrossing through clusters of thick forest.

The trail tested hikers' true grit as the wandering path transformed into a steep dangling precipice of loose mud and rocks. Scaling boulders and squeezing through narrow strips of unobstructed ground was a tightrope gamble. Jake and Susan guided each other's footsteps as they peregrinated the pass.

Hours later, Susan and Jake nearly collapsed, panting, desperate for oxygen. Five miles of backcountry hiking made them curse and bless the ground as the pain of tackling the climb nearly killed them; the raw beauty and tapestry of natural beauty provided inspiration for living.

"Is it physically possible to be exhausted and invigorated at the same time?" Susan's heart roared with adrenaline. "The trail is harsh. The road is narrow. The valley is far, and the rocks are steep. Ironic how we search for peace in the wild abandon, even stranger that we find reconciliation in the isolation."

"Hiking is a supernatural endeavor," Jake said, staring into the mystical landscape of the wilderness, its secrets whispering stories of fire and ice. "Hiking is the crossroads of the physical and spiritual realms. You can set off on a hike, weak of spirit. In the climb, you discover strength in your struggle with the mountain. The climb transcends the pain and hardship, creating a metamorphosis. You discover humility and empowerment. You are frail and strong. Those who set off on the trail full of ego will be broken, and in the fracture a chance for growth and reflection occurs."

"No act restrains and frees you more than hiking," Susan reflected. "The climb nearly tears your knees apart. It is grueling. Even the best boots can't prevent your ankles from swelling as you walk on tiptoe afoot the tree roots, gravel, and slippery slopes. The lungs nearly fail before adapting, determined to utilize the sparse oxygen to empower the body to keep living. The heart finds its beat in the rhythm of the forest. You are willing to rest in the chaos and find your footing even in the most treacherous paths. Just when you think you're broken, you find an inner push to take one more step, then another. If you stop walking, you stiffen up. You must move, your body needs to keep climbing, survival kicks in, and in that battle between cursing and blessing the ground, you accept endurance. You find a restless peace. And in that peace, you recognize rocks as statues and the cliffs as bridges and the trees as doors, with the sky a window to heaven."

"I can hardly complain about climbing a few difficult miles when you consider the eons of geologic history and divine creativity it took to imagine this space into reality." Jake pointed to a nearby two-ton boulder that was so perfectly placed, it resembled a gargoyle guardian clenching its teeth into the mountain. "The uplift and orchestrated chaos it took to form this unbridled refuge is a reminder that our suffering in this realm is not the end of design, but a divergent path creating something beautiful even out of destruction and pain."

The backcountry scenery cast an enchantment on Jake and Susan, luring them to run into unspoken territory. They fell into a quiet trance as they stared into the heart of the canyon below.

"It's called Echo Canyon because if you speak into the canyon's ear, it echoes back a reply. Legend has it that the echo reflects your past meeting your future. Mountaineers often are reminded of their mistakes and triumphs through the echo's roar. The echo isn't a voice of regret but hope to learn from the past and let go." Jake was desperate and hopeful in his desire for rebuilding a future with Susan from the echo of their past.

"The past has a way of rearing its ugly head, but it is only an echo. You don't have to listen to its call. The echo is a choice we don't have to obey." Susan spoke boldly as she reflected on her memories like the dance of shadow and light against the canyon gate. She thought of Bradley, an echo haunting her mind so sharp she let them sting. As Susan peered into the depths of the canyon, she discovered another layer in the art of letting go. "When the voices rage inside your head, you can either listen in and converse with ghosts or tune out the noise as interference, until the wind dies down and your mind is at peace."

"It's a liberating realization."

Susan and Jake roared shouts into the canyon, the chasm answering back, bold, like an invitation. A brief silence fell between Susan and Jake as they ruminated on the past and dangled on the precipice of their future. The sounds of silence were wild as a whisper, sharp as a warning, and the wind rustled the trees as the magpie cawed.

"Why did you shut me out years ago?" Susan blurted out, demanding an explanation. "You refused to talk to me for years. We were best friends. I don't understand why you disappeared."

"You were married, and I was busy with work." Jake was shocked and at the same time relieved by the question.

"Darn it, Jake, after everything, are you still going to play this game?"

"What do you want me to say, Susan? You eloped, ran off to Seattle, and I had a life at the lake."

"Don't play that card when you know I'm talking about the fracture before I got married." Susan let her emotions erupt like the Yellowstone Caldera. "I loved you long before I ever met Bradley Dixon."

"You married Bradley," Jake shouted, his voice reverberating like hailstones in the canyon.

"I married Bradley because you rejected me. You told me point-blank, 'Susan, I don't love you.'"

"I always loved you, Susan. You're a fool not to realize that."

"You never uttered the words *I love you*. Not until today. You broke my heart."

"Funny, I could say the same thing about you," Jake said, defensive. "You ran off and married Bradley Dixon, of all forsaken people. You gave up on us."

"That night at Storm Point, the rain pounding down against the lightning and the thunder…I held you in my arms and begged you to be honest with me. I confessed my love for you. I thought you loved me, I wanted to marry you, to have a life at the lake together, but you pushed me away. You said you didn't love me beyond friendship. I was devastated. If I gave up on us, you are guilty of letting me run away."

"I did that to release you."

"Don't put this on me. You were afraid."

"I despised Bradley because he loved you. He owned your heart."

"You had my heart, and you threw it away." Tears fell hard down Susan's cheeks. "I told you that if you loved me, I would forsake my engagement to Bradley. I poured my heart out and you refused my love. You gave me your permission to marry Bradley. I should have trusted my gut, I should have fought for us, but I was angry and broken when you pushed me away. What was I supposed to do?"

"Susan, wasn't it obvious I was lying? I loved you then and I am in love with you now. I pushed you away because I loved you. I thought you were in love with Bradley. I guess I thought he was better for you—he had money and ambition. I never wanted anything but to marry you and live at the lake. Bradley promised me that he would make you happy. He swore to the moon that he would never hurt you. He begged me to give up my stake in your heart so that you and he could build a life together."

"I did love Bradley, but he was never the keeper of my heart. He was a spare, a boy waiting in the wings to sweep me off my feet when you walked away."

"I'm sorry," Jake said, starting to recognize his mistakes.

"I'm broaching this now because I am in love with you. I don't want us to go back down that precarious path again. I don't want your heart, or mine, to get twisted in stubborn fear. I'm still raw, grieving the turmoil of the last eight months. I'm fragmented. The healing process might take time. I want to be with you. If we're going to take a chance on romance, I want to do it right. Let's take our time. Understand that I'm in repair. I can't trust myself half the time, but I trust our love. I want it to grow and to embrace the process of falling back into our love."

"I love you." Jake discovered freedom and power in the words. "I promise that I won't let fear divide us again. I will be patient. Just being close to you is the air I breathe and the blood through my veins."

"We'll take it slow, building a strong foundation, not a castle of sand?"

"'Patiently I hope, silently I take, lonely our hearts, the sun will break.'" Jake recited another one of Susan's high school poems.

They sat on the ledge, the echoes of the past finally charging their hearts to find understanding and hope, not in their failings, but in second chances.

Chapter 21

July's tourism rush left little time for Jake and Susan to be alone. They stole moments in between shifts, desperate for one another's company: tenderly strolling on the shores of the lake at twilight, sharing kettle corn at the farmer's market, trekking to Storm Point with the Hidden Creek Hiking Society under the full moon, kayaking to Kootenai Point… Those golden moments pulled their heart strings.

It did not take long for the Arnett clan to wise up to the fact that Susan and Jake were an item.

"You're spending a lot of time running around with Susan *Dixon*," Molly said, hard-nosed.

"We enjoy each other's company." Jake gave an impatient shrug. It was a mutual decision to delay announcing their relationship officially until after Susan finished her contract at the lodge in late August.

"I saw you tangled up like star-crossed lovers kissing in the heat of the Fourth of July barn dance." Molly was transparent in her disapproval.

"We did kiss." Jake dismissed it as no more than a change in the weather.

"Be careful. Cupid's arrow is a sharp-edged weapon. It can bring you to your knees in love, simultaneously breaking your heart," Molly warned.

"It's a risk worth taking. For the first time in years, I'm happy. If my heart winds up broken, it's mine to mend. Let me be happy."

On the third weekend in July, hundreds of model-boat enthusiasts converged at the Solitude Lake Lodge for the Wind Drinker Festival. A tradition for thirty years, hobbyists entered their model boats in two jam-packed days of races. There were various competition class levels, from motorized to non-motorized craft, size categories, children and adult races, most creative boat, and more.

Susan called on the expertise of area woodworker George Hull to assist her Explorers in building a junior sailboat for the races. The campers divided into several teams, working together to design their watercraft.

The Young Buckaroos engineered a pirate ship, propelled by sails and a small motor. Susan was impressed with the mechanical ability of the young kids. They listened intently to instructions, avidly putting together their masterpiece with out-of-the-box ideas. Their boat would compete in the children's race that gave a different prize to all participants.

The Lone Rangers drew a line in the sand as a fierce competition between boys versus girls emerged. The girls architected a river showboat, while the boys opted for a battleship-inspired motor craft.

The Running Eagles, divided into two co-ed teams, worked on a Lewis and Clark–inspired keelboat and a replica of the Glacier National Park iconic scenic wood boats that float on the park's many spectacular lakes.

Jake, Gilligan, and Russell also put their hats into the competition. Gilligan put his back behind the S.S. *Minnow II*.

"Might as well be putting money in the *Titanic*," Jake kidded. "The idea is to sail the boat, not crash into a desert isle."

"The *Titanic* crashed into an iceberg; the original *Minnow* washed up on a tropical paradise. This three-hour tour will be a success. You have Gilligan's oath on that."

"That doesn't reassure me."

"The *Minnow* can outwit your schooner any day."

"The *Larkspur* is an elegant ship that will fly past the competition."

"Not if my *Dutchman* has anything to say about it," Russell argued.

The Wind Drinker Festival kicked off Friday night with a fish fry, water plunge, and kayak race. Jake and Susan caught up over a dinner of steamed rainbow trout, hushpuppies, and fried okra.

"My dad and I entered the junior race when I was twelve," Susan recalled. "He was set on engineering and blueprints to ensure our boat would have speed and power. I was more concerned with having the boat look awesome. In the end, we compromised on a corvette theme. The boat came in third place. I still have the medal hung proudly in the Lone Moose study."

"I was so jealous. You had the coolest boat on the water, while my starship boat sank just after liftoff."

"The concept of a Star Destroyer boat was cool, but like the Empire, it was overpowered by the Force…"

"Force of gravity, wind, engineering…nothing worked with that boat." Jake cracked a smile. "This year things will be different. The *Larkspur* will ride the waves of competition, rushing to first place."

"Not if Gilligan has anything to say about it. He's been handing out "Team *Minnow*" buttons all week." Susan's laugh was so full of joy. It was a release to laugh so purely. "I'm looking forward to the Explorers' boats. We worked long and hard to bring their ideas to life."

Caught up in the sunset, a cool breeze dancing off the water, the couple leaned in for a kiss.

"Fly! Ride the wind," Susan shouted, cheering for the Buckaroos' pirate ship. Twenty-five entries in the children's race rushed down the lake as kids navigated their ships towards the finish line. Families were in a frenzy, rooting their favorite Buckaroo on. In the end, the Solitude pirate ship finished second. The reward: a pizza party at the lodge, and T-shirts.

The Lone Ranger Showdown was a down-to-the-wire race for first place. The battleship roared ahead, only to be overtaken by the girls showboat in the final minute. The ships were neck and neck across the finish line. It was so close that the judge nearly declared a tie, but the showboat eked by to take home first place. Both teams won medallions, T-shirts, and gift certificates to the Lodge Gift Shop.

The Lone Ranger Snowdown teams mounted valiant efforts. The Lewis and Clark keelboat came in second place, and the Glacier Park Boat replica was a strong third-place finisher. Each team received Solitude Lake Lodge gift baskets and medals to commend their efforts.

The competition resumed at noon, after a pig pickin' and ice-cream social. Twenty races in varying classes rushed the water in hopes of winning a piece of the Wind Drinker crown. Fast-paced action, creative boats, and miniature to giant models captured the fascination of onlookers, each rooting from the shore for their favorite ship.

The intensity of the races came to a thrilling end with the Solitude Cup Finals. Jake, Gilligan, and Russell competed against thirty-five other finalists, withered down from the original two hundred entrants.

The *Dutchman* flipped over early on, skimming the water on its side before breaking apart.

"Dang it." Russell's face was deep red, showing his annoyance.

"The *Minnow II* and *Larkspur* are holding steady in the top five," Molly observed.

"Shoot, the *Minnow* lost a propeller; it's veering to the left and losing speed." A few minutes later the *Minnow* crashed on shore.

"I blame the skipper," Gilligan said, furious at the crash.

The *Larkspur* rocketed to second place, struggling to dash past last year's boat winner—*Sir Galahad*.

"Team Jake!!!" The lodge staff erupted with encouragement. In a thrilling finish, the *Larkspur* jolted ahead for an underdog victory.

"Congratulations!" Susan embraced Jake.

"Victory is sweet—" Jake held up his trophy "—when I have you standing beside me."

The lodge hosted a banquet dinner and wine tasting for adults, while the Explorers enjoyed oven-fire pizza in the Lewis Center while watching *Treasure Island* and *Robinson Crusoe*.

Chapter 22

The last two weeks of July blazed to torrid temperatures, as the dry air coupled with the blistering sun left the region subject to wildfires. Missoula Smokejumpers battled flames in in the Lolo National Forest, fifty miles south of Hidden Creek. Three days of torrential rain, a rarity in Montana summer, dissipated the rapid spread of the damage. The firefighters were able to contain the boundaries to four thousand acres of forest in the Missoula area.

"The fire was sparked by a bolt of lightning," local news affiliates reported.

Montana's dry heat was known for igniting dramatic lightning storms in the prairies just south of Seeley Lake. On the surface, fire was a destructive power, decimating forests with the force of dragon's breath. The aftermath was devastating, yet despite the fury, fire was a life-sustaining element in the forest. It strengthened the forest by clearing overgrowth and unhealthy trees. The aspen tree had evolved to release seeds when the forest was on fire, naturally reseeding forests that were healthier and sustainable for the next generation. Lodge pole pines and ponderosa were fire resistant. The clearing tore down pine beetle–infested trees that clogged up the vitality of healthy trees. Fire, a deadly spark, could only temporarily destroy a landscape. In time, the scenery and biodiversity of the ecosystem was refined by fire.

Susan meditated on wildfire, finding comfort in the resiliency of the trees, particularly aspen. The tree was a symbol of hope in turmoil. Individual aspens lived up to 150 years aboveground, but the root system of the tree colony was long-lived. In some cases, it was sustained for thousands of years, sending up new trunks as older trunks died off aboveground. Ancient forest met new beginning. The deep roots were protected from the heat of fire, with new sprouts being triggered to grow after fire burned out. A foundation that could survive the worst of crises, with growth and adaptability to adjust to the change.

Each day, Susan contended with buried emotions, scalded by grief and anger. It was hidden, tucked in the shadows of the day. In some ways Susan was like a fire, aflame with rage, circumstances often smoky. Yet from the ashes she rose, like a phoenix, learning new lessons. The foundation of faith and hope were her stronghold, while she constructed a future not afflicted by a charred past.

Susan remembered that ash was a symbol of penitence, and redemption can be found in even the scorched earth. She turned her worry inside out and over thread by thread to God.

She also battled the fire in her heart—a smoldering torch for Jake Arnett. Susan rattled her brain looking for reasons to end the romance that she was sure would crash and burn. In the end, the joy and peace of their spare moments together kept her head above water. Her love for Jake was a sweet release. They would tread carefully, respecting their fragile hearts. Yet to deny the opportunity for love on the presumption of failure during trial, Susan knew that argument was fear.

"I'm not giving in to fear."

"I saw the write-up in today's edition of the *Missoulian* about this weekend's Hidden Creek Festival of the Arts. It gives kudos to the volunteers and artists on starting up this Montana homegrown event," Susan mentioned to Marion McCloud over a cup of coffee at Marmot Books.

"The *Lively Times*, *Daily Inter-Lake* and *Bozeman Daily Chronicle* are doing write-ups as well," Marion noted before sipping on her latte.

For the past six months, a board of twelve local volunteers, helmed by Bird Woman Art Gallery owner Marion McCloud, had invested their time into planning the first annual arts festival. The mission was to promote local artists and foster cultural opportunities.

Susan had jumped on as a volunteer in mid-May to assist with children's activities. She'd worked out a deal with Molly for the Solitude Lake Lodge to serve as a festival partner, providing the Lewis Center and barn for the Missoula Children's Theatre workshops and rehearsals.

The Missoula Children's Theatre was an internationally recognized company that provided a traveling theater camp for kids. For more than forty years, with a focus on creativity and teamwork, the organization had given children the chance to participate in a weeklong theater project, under the guidance of MCT theater professionals. The result: over sixty-five thousand kids would be cast in one of many MCT International Tour shows from Missoula and beyond.

The MCT representatives, Tess and Carol, arrived in Hidden Creek the Monday before the festival. That day an open audition for *The Secret Garden* took place at the Solitude Lake Lodge in the barn. All fifty-two aspiring actors, kids from as far north as Bigfork and as far south as Seeley Lake, were cast in the musical. Solitude Lake's sponsorship of the presenting fees for Missoula Children's Theatre meant that the camp was free to all participants.

Over the next five days, MCT helmed four-and-a-half-hour focused rehearsals. Students learned lines, staging, movements, and theater skills in a vibrant and nurturing atmosphere. Three enrichment workshops provided interactive instruction on a variety of theater topics.

Susan enjoyed supervising the immense talent and creativity of the K–12 performers. Throughout the week, shy, aloof children began to find confidence in their talent, shining onstage and among friends. The bonds made between the kids and adults that week would last a lifetime.

"You'll be astounded by the knack these kids have for putting on a show," Susan unabashedly bragged of the MCT participants.

"MCT does an amazing job with bringing the arts alive to children in communities across the nation," Marion agreed.

"They're performing *The Secret Garden*?" Lacy stepped in, refilling Susan's decaf coffee. "That's a magical story. One of my favorite books."

"Mine too." Susan smiled. "The mystery, romance, and atmosphere of that book is a journey of self-discovery. I read it a dozen times as a child."

"I'm stoked that Montana Shakespeare in the Parks is making a stop at the festival. It'll be the first time I've seen *Two Gentlemen of Verona* onstage."

"We were fortunate that Shakes was available to perform at our festival," Marion enthused. "They're a high-demand performance company."

"My cousin, Andrea performed in the company during her tenure at Montana State. She portrayed Ophelia in *Hamlet* and Lady Macbeth in the Scottish play," Keeley added in.

"She is a drama queen. That's a compliment." Lacy smiled.

"The company has a forty-plus-year history dating back to 1973. They're the only professional touring company in the United States to reach extensively to rural areas. This summer alone they're hitting sixty communities with *Two Gentlemen of Verona* and *Othello*, spanning into remote Montana, western North Dakota, northern Wyoming, Idaho and eastern Washington. Its rural and small-town focus allows communities to be exposed to top theater that would otherwise not be afforded the opportunity."

"What Andrea loved about performing with Shakes is that they have a focus on youth theater. In the summer they have workshops to accompany performances. While in the winter, they bring Shakespeare into Montana schools. It's a true gem."

"What's the status on arts and craft vendors?" Susan inquired.

"Eighty artisans from across Montana, Idaho, and Washington have signed up, each with unique styles from pottery to grass baskets, photography to paintings, Native American expressions, and jewelry—a diverse arts market," Marion informed them. "The food trucks are nonprofit vendors, each with connections to the arts in the Flathead, Swan, and Clearwater Valleys."

"The children's activities booth will have free face painting and scrap-metal art. Nettie volunteered to lead a storytelling session featuring Montana folk legends," Susan said.

The friends and festival planners continued to chat over coffee for fifteen minutes before heading to Belton Park to finish setup. In the past forty-eight hours, the expansive city park had been transformed into a small arts mecca, with countless artisans setting up shop, the tech crew readying the Art Stage, and volunteers bustling as they set up retail and food booths.

The festival kicked off tonight with the Friday Night Art Walk. Downtown shops would stay open late, showcasing the best of Hidden Creek, while jazz and roots musicians would perform street corner symphonies.

Saturday and Sunday would offer festivalgoers an eclectic itinerary of activities, in addition to the arts market and food trucks. Children's activities, lessons in the art of fly tying by Mystic Outfitters, a photography exhibit sponsored by the historical society, a dance performance by Swan Ballet, Missoula Children's Theatre, and two performances by Montana Shakespeare in the Parks.

Setup wound down just after seven o'clock. Volunteers were treated to a pizza dinner under the oak trees in Belton Square, a creekside picnic area in the park. Susan snuck out early to join Jake and Keeley on the Art Walk.

"Everything raring to go for tomorrow?" Jake inquired.

"Finger and face paints, scrap metals, glues, and construction paper—we have it covered."

"The kids are going to have a blast," Keeley remarked. "I'm a proud mother of two of the stars."

"I appreciate the lodge for supporting the festival."

"The arts are the lifeblood of a society. Seeing the kids interact this week during rehearsals was priceless. I can't wait to see our young actors take the stage."

"My camera is charged and ready to take a zillion pictures. I know they'll take the audience by storm."

"Speaking of kids, I'm due to meet Holden and the boys at the law office. Catch you later?"

Jake and Susan held hands as they strolled slowly down Main and Front Streets, taking in the ambiance of the avant-garde jazz coupled with the purple sky as they peeked into shops. While perusing Yogo Jewelry, cup of wine in hand, Susan was drawn to a striking silver necklace inlaid with colorful handblown glass.

"Such artistry." Susan admired the piece.

"This necklace is made from Montana sterling silver, and antique glass, by a Livingston, Montana, artist. It's a unique piece," Miller McCloud detailed. "Would you like to try it on?"

"I couldn't possibly afford it." Susan bit her lip. Since near bankruptcy, buying jewelry was off the table. Still, she could dream a little.

"Go on, try it on," Miller and Jake encouraged.

"It doesn't hurt to dream for a moment." Susan latched the piece around her neck.

"You look stunning." Jake complimented.

"It compliments your features," Miller agreed.

"It is a lovely necklace."

"I'd be happy to work out a deal, a payment plan?" Miller offered.

"Thank you for the offer, but I'm on a fiscal cliff budget right now." Susan's tone was positive. She had shied away from feeling deprivation. In dire straits she had learned what was important: food, shelter, and love. The necklace was nice, but she couldn't justify spending $300 of her savings for a trinket that would be stuck in a jewelry box most of the year.

"I'll keep it on hold a few more days, just in case you change your mind," Miller offered. Best friends with Kip Blanchard, the jeweler had known Susan since she was a tot. He would have given her the necklace for free to see her happy, but Miller knew Susan was too stubborn to accept it without cost.

Susan and Jake ambled down to the Swan Valley Pharmacy to whet their sweet tooth.

"Howdy," Karen Kincaid greeted the couple. "The town is all abuzz with the arts festival. I'm looking forward to exploring the arts and crafts tomorrow."

"I just hope that my wife keeps the budget in tow," Phil kidded.

"We had a hankering for your world-famous huckleberry milkshake."

"Coming right up."

The friends caught up while enjoying dessert.

"It's great to see a smile on your face, Blancher," Karen noted. She had been worried about Susan's recovery.

"Her smile lights up the night," Jake agreed.

"Your mom keeps pressing me to get you to come for a weekend visit to Missoula." Karen remained in close contact with Beatrix Blanchard.

"I needed some time to get settled into the Lone Moose. I'm planning a visit at the end of September."

Susan loved her mother dearly, and certainly wasn't putting her off. Her mother had been a rock during this trial. The foundation of support that she desperately needed. Beatrix Blanchard worried constantly about her daughter. She understood the loss of a husband and was livid at Bradley's betrayal.

Susan's decision to delay her visit to September was twofold. She needed time to stand on her own two feet, while acclimating to her new life in Hidden Creek. Her job at the lodge left little time for travel, even ninety minutes south to

Missoula. Beatrix had offered to visit her in Hidden Creek, but knowing that her mother, prone to inertia, despised the winding drive on the Seeley to Swan, Susan instead suggested a long weekend visit in late September. If things continued to go well with Jake, Susan hoped to bring him along for the visit.

"My friend Lisa, from Seattle, called this morning with a surprise," Susan shared. "She's coming to visit next week."

"It will be marvelous to meet her," Karen enthused.

"She is a character—Seattle's best real estate agent."

"As long as she isn't trying to convince you to move out of Hidden Creek," Jake firm "I don't want to lose you."

"My future is squarely in the Lone Moose," Susan averred. "It'll be fun to have her in town."

"Bring her by the pharmacy for milkshakes on the house."

"That's an offer no one can refuse." Susan smiled.

Thousands filled Belton Park for the Hidden Creek Festival of the Arts on Saturday and Sunday. The aroma of carnival foods and area food trucks sweetened the air. Patrons perused the hubbub of artisans in the interactive demonstration corner—cracking the pottery wheel, sanding and chopping wood, welding steel—and there was the flutter of chatter as shoppers bought crafts. The anticipation of theater performances on the main stage made for an exciting weekend.

Except for a small lunch break, Susan manned the children's booth all day Saturday and Sunday. Hundreds of children ranging in ages from preschool to teens waited in line to have their faces painted. Nettie engaged young minds with her knack for storytelling The scrap art turned into a unique display of creativity in motion.

The Missoula Children's Theatre was the highlight of Saturday's performance lineup. The crowd roared in applause to commemorate a job well done to the gifted young actors.

On Sunday afternoon Shakespeare in the Parks delighted audiences to the comedy *The Two Gentlemen of Verona*. Susan was a self-professed "Bardophile," eager to teach Shakespeare at the high school level. The difficulty with Shakespeare was the language curve. The language sounded formal but was vernacular of the day, albeit with the intellectual genius and finesse that only the Bard could provide. Montana Shakespeare in the Parks staged the performances in a way that brought the language and characters alive. The audience was able to determine the plot, motivations, agony, and joy taking place onstage from the strong caliber of the cast and crew.

With the festival winding down at six o'clock, Susan stayed behind to help with teardown. The last weekend of July had gone off with a bang. A successful festival that brought the community together, while serving as a tourism driver. She looked forward to volunteering again next year.

Chapter 23

Susan looked at the calendar. August 1. Had time slipped by so quickly? In three weeks, her contract with the Solitude Lake Lodge would be up. In just over a month, she would be starting her new position at Hidden Creek High School. Suddenly she was overwhelmed.

August invigorated her senses, the last gasp of summer, powerful and fierce beauty...yet September was an unknown beast. She had grown accustomed to the pace of summer, her work at the lodge, sitting on the docks with Jake. August would be eclipsed in a breath, and she feared that she would be swallowed up in a cold, unsteady future. Winter. It was a word that was a curse to speak of in Montana summer, yet it was on the tip of her tongue. She feared the shift in the seasons.

Plotting the month's schedule, she counted the days and weeks, anxious. Four weeks of work, preparing for the fall semester, errands...and August 25...her thirty-eighth birthday. The thought of being two years short of forty was a half-glass scenario—she was happy to be under the hill, but scared that she was officially approaching middle age. Getting older had never bothered Susan until now. For the first time, it felt scary.

Susan buried the emotions—she would rejoice in the final weeks of summer, even if the bitter cold of the unknown lay ahead.

"Lisa!" Susan beamed, overjoyed to see her friend.

"You look fantastic." Lisa was pleased to see the glow in her friend's cheeks. She suspected that Jake Arnett was responsible for the reemergence of Susan's smile.

"How was the drive from Spokane?" Lisa chose to break up the long drive, with an overnight stay with family in Spokane.

"Gorgeous…lost in the wilderness. I understand why they call this God's country—every mile, from the barest plain to tallest mountain, is filled with awe-inspiring beauty," Lisa said as she stepped inside the Lone Moose. "This is a bucolic hideaway. Solitude indeed. The remoteness and stillness of the lake. I'm enamored."

"I am ecstatic that you're here." Susan put the kettle on.

"Communication has been sparse on your end. I wanted to check up on you. I miss you."

"Lone Moose rules: no working, and since cell reception is nonexistent, your clients will have to wait a few days."

"You have Wi-Fi," Lisa teased. "For the record, I plan to spend the next four days blissfully unaware of the outside world, enjoying a much-needed vacation, spending as much time with my best friend as possible. I'm eager to meet the mysterious Jake Arnett."

Susan tried to remain tight-lipped about her relationship with Jake. Still, the way she gushed in emails about time spent with her old flame, Lisa sensed that romance was in the air.

"I've arranged for us to have dinner tomorrow night at the Solitude Lake Lodge after my shift."

Over the next hour, the friends enjoyed a gabfest over a pot of rooibos tea accompanied with Flathead cherry crumb cake, both engrossed in the latest details of their lives. Susan was curious about Seattle happenings, while Lisa grilled her about life in Hidden Creek.

"I don't want to smother you with questions, but how are you doing?" Lisa inquired. "Don't give me the blasé 'I'm fine,' sweep-it-under-the-rug answer. You have been through a traumatic experience. Doldrums, melancholy, griping, complaining, or jubilation—I'm here to listen and hopefully offer sound advice, or at least commiserate with you."

"I came to Solitude Lake broken, trying to survive the crash and clamor of my day-to-day existence. Bradley left a vacancy in my heart, his actions a stab wound that hit me from behind. I compare it to being in a disaster zone. My time at the lake has given me a newfound perspective. I'm still in survival mode, but the peace I've found in God and in this majestic scenery is allowing me to heal. It might be an iota of repair, but I feel revitalized. I don't know what the future holds, but I'm fully aware that I will move forward. I will never fully get over Bradley's death and duplicity, but I will reconcile it and find peace to forgive and release that burden of anger."

"It can take a lifetime to heal and to forgive. It can be piecemeal at times. Funny how a splinter can break so much skin. The skin becomes calloused before the new untarnished layers emerge. What matters is that you keep yourself open to that process. Allow love and forgiveness to break down walls of despair while building a foundation of trust, faith, and hope."

Susan prepared a Mexican-themed dinner as Lisa settled into the guest room. The worry of her mounting to-do list was cleared instantly by the comforting presence of her friend.

The brilliant shift between nocturne, the stars and moon dipping behind the mountains, eclipsed by the rising sun, created a supernatural aura of color and light.

Susan and Lisa greeted the morning on the back porch, dining on fritter cakes and hot chocolate, before setting off on an early hike to Hidden Creek Falls.

Lisa wasn't an outdoor gal. Her niche was finding off-the-wall coffee joints in Seattle, roaming Pike Place Market, snacking on Chukar Cherries, and occasionally window-shopping in Fremont art galleries. Her primary exercise was pounding the pavement on the real estate trail or mall-walking in Bellevue.

But even city slicker Lisa could not deny the tranquility of an early-morning hike. The sound of rushing water, the damp dew on the forest floor, the chirping of birds—it was a true escape from the hustle and bustle of her day-to-day life.

"My kids would be in heaven here, playing outside and swimming on the lake."

"They're free to visit anytime. Winter break would be ideal for cross-country skiing."

"You have a better affinity for winter than I do. The thought of snow makes me numb." Lisa shivered. "The cold damp days in Seattle get under my skin. I cannot imagine negative temps and ten feet of snow. Skiing is not in my vocabulary."

"I tend to agree. Winter isn't my season. But I'll put up with the frigid temps if the reward is sublime summers."

"Montana summers are divine. If only we could bottle up the sunshine for a cloudy day."

"If only." Susan sighed.

After the hike, Susan showered and changed.

"I'm headed to work. Feel free to help yourself to anything in the kitchen. Towels are in the hall closet if you want to go for a swim. Remember the Lone Moose rules—relax and have fun."

"I'll restrain myself from working too hard," Lisa swore. "Meet you at the lodge at six?"

"Look forward to it."

The hectic pace of the day flew past, guided by the boundless energy of Solitude Explorers partaking in water polo, watercolor painting, and volleyball. The first week of

August was the last full week of the program, as many K–12 students and families were readying to go back to school mid-August to early September. Instead of seven days of camp itineraries, the lodge would offer programs Thursday–Sunday.

Susan savored the moment, enjoying the simple peace that children's laughter and imagination can provide. To be young and hopeful, set on dreams.

Finishing her shift just after five o'clock, she changed out of her muddy shorts and lodge polo shirt into a colorful print shirt and pair of khakis from Patagonia. Checking her appearance in the mirror, she smacked her lips with balm and flushed her cheeks. Despite layering on SPF 100, the intense high-altitude sun left her with sun-kissed skin.

She hoped that Lisa would like Jake and vice versa. It was strange to have two different worlds collide. So much of Susan's Seattle life had been ripped away from her present reality. It was a ghost. It was hard to grasp that the Lone Moose was her home now, not just a summer hideaway. Her house in Queen Anne was no longer her own. There was a disconnect.

"You look sharp," Jake complimented, kissing Susan on the cheek.

"Nice to see you out of Wranglers and that forsaken plaid button-up shirt you insist on wearing, even though it has holes," Susan jested.

"It's a lucky shirt." Jake defended. "Where's Lisa?"

"Right here." Lisa stormed into the lodge lobby, her gregarious personality in tow. "You weren't kidding when you touted Jake's good looks. He is a handsome catch."

"Aw, shucks." Jake revealed his signature smile.

"A little rough around the edges, but he cleans up nicely." Susan put her arm around Jake. "I'm fortunate to have him in my life."

"I'm the lucky one. I don't hold a flicker of a flame compared to Susan. She's a true catch," Jake voiced. It was obvious, the way the pair looked at one another, that they were head over heels in love. Lisa was thrilled to see Susan so happy.

She hoped that this love would grow deeper roots than a haphazard summer fling.

Solitude Dining Room was always packed. In addition to lodge guests, hungry diners traveled for upwards of fifty miles to sample Chef Aaron's award-winning cuisine.

With an hour until their reservation window, they carved out a corner of the spirited saloon, toasting their glasses to adventure and friendship Lisa opted for the Yogo Sapphire Martini, a dash of huckleberry vodka and juice. Jake, not a huge drinker, decided to go with a Moscow Mule in a copper mug, while Susan stuck with her standby: one glass of cabernet and a glass of lemon-spritzed water.

"Susan says that you've been best friends since childhood?"

"Inseparable since we were toddlers. Although Susan was more of a troublemaker in preschool than I was."

"That is a lie! You nearly drove your dad's tractor into the lake when we were four. We flew down the hill before the car stalled. Thank God we only moved the gears to Neutral."

"Face it, Blancher, you were just as culpable, albeit your cute face and dimples got you out of time-out. My dad refused to let me touch his tractor again until I was fifteen. He's still a little leery of letting me drive anything but his rusted Chevy."

Witnessing the dynamic energy between the couple, Lisa wondered why Susan had failed to mention Jake in Seattle. Did they have a falling-out? She curbed her curiosity. Susan deserved her secrets.

"Clue me into your history? How did you become friends?" Jake asked Lisa.

"Susan and I met while volunteering at the Woodland Park Zoo in Seattle at a Halloween trick or treat event. Susan was dressed up as Dorothy from *The Wizard of Oz* and I was the Wicked Witch of the West."

"She threatened to set her flying monkeys on me."

"Only after your sinister promise to melt me with the bucket of water in your hand."

"In spite of our differences, we managed to find common ground. We've been friends ever since, through the good times and the bad."

"Our reservation is up," Jake said as the buzzer went off.

"Good thing—I'm famished." Susan hadn't eaten anything since breakfast.

The hostess led the party to a secluded table overlooking the lake, the fiery sun in glorious color before surrendering to night.

Looking over the menu, Lisa opted for the Cowboy Filet, a succulent Montana grass-fed cut of beef drizzled in cabernet sauce, with grilled mushrooms, blackened onions, a Manhattan baked potato, and house salad with vinaigrette. Susan ordered the half-size pork tenderloin with wild rice and green beans. Jake settled on a grilled chicken sandwich with house-made kettle chips.

"This food is amazing." Lisa was impressed. "This steak can hold a torch above even the best steakhouses in Seattle. That is no easy feat."

"Chef Aaron is a gem. He's earned accolades from the *New York Times*, *Wine Spectator*, *Sunset Magazine*, and more."

"This baked potato is massive."

"It isn't just any baker, it's a Manhattan baker," Susan held. "Manhattan, Montana, that is. The potato capital of the world."

For dessert the trio split a Super Volcano chocolate cake, with decadent fudge flowing as you cut into the moist torte shell.

"I haven't been this stuffed since Thanksgiving." Lisa set down her fork. "And frankly, this meal outshines my dry attempt at roasting turkey."

"Lisa isn't a cook."

"Sad but true. Susan and I took a baking class at the community college. Susan's cake resembled a photo from Martha Stewart. Mine erupted in the oven, too much baking soda apparently, causing a small fire and a building evacuation.

My boyfriend told me that if I ever cook without his supervision, I'll be fined a hefty liability waiver."

"You are quite the character, just like Susan described. It's been wonderful having you at the lake."

"You aren't rid of me yet. I'm here for forty-eight more hours."

"We better take advantage of every second." Susan raised the last sip of wine in her glass.

The next day, Lisa hung out at the lodge, assisting Susan with the Solitude Explorers.

"You've done a stand-up job with this program," Lisa commended. "It's hard to find kid-friendly vacations for the entire family. Solitude Lake's integrated focus from Young Buckaroos to adult activities is an asset."

"It is a special place "

Closing the Lewis Center at four o'clock, Susan and Lisa drove into Hidden Creek, where they toured the small close-knit community. While strolling city blocks, Susan detailed Hidden Creek's colorful history, taking time to introduce Lisa to locals.

They stopped by the Swan Valley Pharmacy, where Karen Kincaid treated the gals to huckleberry milkshakes, welcoming Lisa to town. For dinner they met up with Beth Matheson, Colby Kessler, and Darcy Evans at the Coyote Grill.

Lisa bonded with the women, picking up conversation as if they had been friends for years. Darcy was particularly keen to give the rundown on all the latest Hidden Creek happenings, while Colby shared details of her latest rafting adventure.

"You could not pay me to gamble against the raging rapids," Lisa expressed. "I'm scared to death that I'll fall into the water, hit my head, and drown."

"It's a risk, but I guarantee that as your guide you'll have a safe and fun tubular adventure," Colby tempted.

"No offense. It seems a little iffy." Lisa hesitated.

"Face your fears," Colby insisted. "If you agree to raft, I'll take you out on the Swan River for free tomorrow morning."

"You are luring me into a death trap," Lisa mulled, dangling curiosity and excitement against the dangers of rafting.

"I'm not a rapid runner either," Susan interjected. "That being said, I have gone on the water with Colby numerous times. She'll put you on a Class I rapid that's safe and fun. I think you should give it a shot. Think how stoked Harry, Joe, and Libby would be to see a picture of their mom rafting."

"What the heck?" Lisa caved. "I'll do it."

"Colby Kessler better make sure that I don't fall out of the raft." Lisa was already doubting her decision to run the Swan River.

"She's a pro." Susan offered reassurance. "Pay close attention to the safety instructions and follow Colby's lead. You'll do great."

"I wish you were coming along for the ride."

"I would hop on a raft in a heartbeat if I could get off work," Susan lamented. "I'll be with you in spirit."

"My ghost will haunt the Lone Moose if I don't come out of this alive."

"Don't be dramatic." Susan poured Lisa a cup of freshly squeezed orange juice.

"Says the one who will be building birdhouses indoors all day."

Susan lent Lisa a pair of old sneakers, waterproof board shorts, and a moisture-wicking long sleeve shirt to wear under the wetsuit rental.

"The stretch of the Swan River you'll be running is calm. I've kayaked there dozens of times."

"I'm trusting you, Susan"

Lisa met up with Colby at the Mountain High Water shop just north of Hidden Creek. Six other paddlers, ranging in age from eight to fifty-eight, were on site for the Class I introductory rafting experience.

"Ready to fight the beast?" Colby challenged as she fitted Lisa in a wetsuit, helmet, and personal floatation device.

"I don't want to fight anything. I'm here to enjoy a leisurely drift down Swan River."

"Don't worry, we won't be hitting the "Wild Mile" today."

"Wild Mile?"

"The stretch between Swan Lake and the river's terminus in Flathead Lake. The river pounds with Class V rapids as you maneuver rocks and debris. It's a thrilling power ride."

"Sounds like a suicide run to me," Lisa said under her breath.

With the rafting team outfitted, Colby spent thirty minutes detailing river safety with proper technique, including holding the paddle with a T Grip, ensuring proper installation of your PFD and helmet, how to paddle, what to do if you fall off the raft, dealing with rapids, and other safety precautions.

The group of adventurers piled into the company van and drove to River Access Road, where Kevin Kessler helped everyone onto the raft. He would be serving as the land guide, following the movements of the raft from the ground, ready to assist in case of an emergency. Colby's fiancé, Zach Turner, would drive the van down to the rendezvous point.

"Remember to sit on the outer tubes. If you sit on the inner cross tubes your paddle will not hit the water," Colby directed. "Keep your toes underneath the cross tube, but not your entire foot—that can lead to injure. If you fall out of the water and we are unable to pick you up with your PFD, remember the defensive swimming and aggressive self-rescue positions. Let's be safe and raise heck on high water."

The group followed Colby's every direction as the raft began to pace down the Swan River. The run was a secluded and quiet float surrounded by brushy forested banks. The fast-moving water riffled, causing just enough turbulence to make Lisa antsy. She kept her focus on Colby, holding a tight T Grip on her paddle, rowing in unison with her fellow rafters.

As they moved downstream, log jams forced the rafting team to maneuver a few difficult turns. The longer they were on the river, the more comfortable the city slicker from Seattle became on the raft. The rumble over small, rough rapids to the long stretches of still water was spectacular fun.

"I had a blast." Lisa commended Colby as she got off the raft at the rendezvous point.

"Ready for the Wild Mile tomorrow?"

Lisa laughed. "Nah, I'll stick with calm waters from here on out."

"I hate that you're leaving tomorrow." Susan expressed her disappointment as the friends huddled around the campfire, roasting marshmallows.

"I'm not that easy to get rid of. I'll visit again soon, with my kids next time."

"They'll be happy to have you back in Seattle."

"It's hard to believe that Harry is going to be a senior this year. Time flies."

"Does he know where he wants to attend college?"

"The University of Washington is the likely choice. He bleeds Husky purple."

"Summer has been but a breath. I'm coming to grips that in just over a month I'll be starting at Hidden Creek High School. I need to start finalizing lesson plans."

"You and Jake have quite a history," Lisa said, treading carefully.

"He's a great friend."

"Don't be daft. Any fool can see that you're in love with him."

There was a short, awkward silence between them. This was the first time Susan had been forced to confront the relationship in such stark terms.

"I do love Jake."

"Then why run from it? He cares deeply for you."

"If anything, I'm a fool rushing in." Susan thinly cloaked her fear with laughter. For the first time since the start of the month, she was apprehensive. Was it a twinge of guilt that she was finally happy again after Bradley's death exiled her to Solitude Lake? Why was panic suddenly setting in?

"There is a strength in being alone, an island fortress rising above the floods of catastrophe. You cling to self-reliance as a shield so that you don't have to risk losing a part of yourself. You guard your heart with a sharp-edged sword. Philosophers might argue this is the triumph of man—being alone and independent. In truth, if you disconnect yourself from love, refusing to carve a piece of your heart out for the benefit of others, being a spouse or a stranger in need of mercy, then your strength is your greatest weakness. Those who cling to the armor of a lonely heart, with fear of the outside, aren't self-reliant, but forsaken to dependence and possession of eremitism. It's a swift slope into the dregs of self-pity and solipsism."

"You're accusing me of being a narcissist?" Susan was horrified by the accusation.

"Your character of compassion and selflessness is anything but narcissistic," Lisa clarified. "In your grieving state, you're unable at times to see the big picture. It's easy to get tripped up on past mistakes or fear of the future when change is happening at a staggering pace. You cope with the mechanism of pushing away love and clinging to loneliness. You're afraid of being happy, because how can you possibly be happy after the death of your husband and the fallout of the estate? Susan, I'm here to tell you that you have a right to be happy. Falling in love with Jake isn't betraying Bradley. If you allow fear to prevent you from seeing this relationship through, you'll be betraying yourself."

"Strange how the guilt and anxiety appeared. For weeks I've fallen into the comfort and safety of Jake's love without fear. Each moment with him an intrepid step into a new world, unrestrained. The emotions building up inside crashed tonight."

"When my jerk of a husband left me to die, I didn't think I could trust another man. Then I met Craig, twelve years after my divorce. I resisted, pushed back against the power of love, reverting to the habit of distrust. God reminded me that love is an open door that fills the heart with light. I knew that Craig was sent to help heal the fragmented pieces. He was broken too. Together we have built a wonderful friendship and love, which in time I hope leads to marriage. Even if our relationship were to end today, I would not regret the chance." Lisa paused. "If I thought you were rushing into a disaster, a rebound relationship that would tear you and Jake apart, then I would not hesitate in forcing you to hit the brakes. But I know that you've loved Jake a long time. You were teenage sweethearts, and if Bradley hadn't come along, you would probably be married today. This isn't some fly-by-night courtship. Take your time and savor each moment together. Don't throw a lit match to the bridge you need to cross. Otherwise, you'll be left to swim a rocky leg to the other side of the shore."

"I love Jake," Susan whispered confidently, fear beginning to subside. "I always have."

Chapter 24

Susan succumbed to the mounting stack of paperwork and textbooks piled high on her desk. With the fall semester looming, she was brushing up on the district's history and English curriculums, preparing fall lesson plans and reviewing the semester's reading list. Invigorated by the opportunity to share her passion for literature and history with students, she was constructing stimulating lectures and classroom activities.

Revisiting the great literary works of the English language kindled her soul. It was like opening a long-forgotten box of mystery and magic found tucked away in the attic.

She immersed herself in the oral traditions of early British legends and poetry, from *Beowulf*, the oldest written epic in the English language, to Chaucer's *Canterbury Tales*. She studied the early American writers who forged a new nation and the poetry of the 1800s, and the romanticism and transcendentalist movement that stirred Nathaniel Hawthorne. Finding herself lost in the pages of these epic tales, a fire kindled her soul.

Susan's thoughts turned to the copy of *Great Expectations* locked in the office safe. It deserved better than being stuffed in a dark hole, a forgotten sentiment, a gift tied to the doomed love that she and Bradley shared.

The theme of *Great Expectations* resonated deeply with Susan. How great her expectations of love and devotion in committing her trust and dedication to Bradley. Despite his flaws and betrayal, she still loved him. So flawed were these expectations when they hit the coldness of reality. The resolution was bleak, sending her back to square one.

Paradoxically, it was her forced retreat from past expectations and unfulfilled ambition that brought Susan back to the naivety of her youth. In her suffering, she had matured to a new level of understanding and hope.

She rested on a favorite quote from the novel.

"Suffering has been stronger than all other teaching, and has taught me to understand what your heart used to be. I have been bent and broken, but—I hope—into a better shape."

Susan's feet danced in the water, tiptoeing in sand, basking in the fervor of the sun. The shift in the wind served as a swift reminder that time waits for no one. She grappled with the fact that in a few hours her summer contract at the lodge would end.

"I have a surprise,' Jake, sneaking up behind her, whispered.

"You have my full attention." Susan wrapped her arms around Jake.

"A meadowlark whistled that you have a birthday coming up in a few days."

"I don't have a clue as to what you're referring." Susan rolled her eyes.

"I want to sweep you off to Glacier National Park for a romantic getaway," Jake explained. "I have Monday and Tuesday nights booked at the Many Glacier Hotel in the northeastern corner of the park. We can relax on the shores of Swiftcurrent Lake, in the shadow of Chief Mountain, and hike to Grinnell Lake on Monday. On Tuesday, we'll tour Going-to-the-Sun Road via the historic Red 'Jammer' Bus."

"I couldn't possibly…" Susan desperately wanted to steal away for a Glacier rendezvous with Jake, but she resisted the urge. She was aware of the cost involved. She didn't want to burden her boyfriend with the cost of a grand escapade.

"I will not take no for an answer." He pulled her heart strings.

"You are my knight in shining armor."

"I'm just a guy in love with an amazing girl."

Spanning the Continental Divide, Glacier National Park was home to one million acres of majestic, pristine wilderness. The landscape was considered the most intact ecosystem in the continental United States. The convergence of the Great Plains to the stiff-ridged vertebrae of the rugged Rocky Mountains, ancient forests, glacial lakes, waterfalls, clusters of wildflowers, and diverse fauna truly justified Glacier as the Crown of the Continent. To the Blackfeet Nation, the region was the Backbone of the World. Indeed, this rigid, lush, and almost supernatural paradise was a foundation of life, whose ecosystems sustained a far greater reach than the park boundaries.

The drive from Hidden Creek to Glacier was a stunning journey into the extreme geology of northwestern Montana. Heading north on Montana Highway 83, the lush thick forests of the Swan Valley opened up into the Flathead Valley. Flathead Lake was the largest natural freshwater lake west of the Mississippi River. Its clear blue waters were practically devoid of pollution.

"It never ceases to amaze me the sheer size and grandeur of Flathead Lake," Susan mentioned to Jake as the scenic byway skirted lakeside vistas. Flathead was home to numerous state parks, campgrounds, and recreation.

"Let's make a date to explore Wild Horse Island before summer breathes its last breath."

"I haven't been there since we were kids."

"Best field trip ever. This almost mythical island, teeming with wild horses, bighorn sheep, mule deer, waterfowl, and raptors…"

"Glen Matheson's brother, Chuck, runs a boat company that ferries tourists to Wild Horse from Bigfork's Marina Cay."

"I know Chuck Matheson. He knows Wild Horse Island inside and out. We'll schedule a tour in the coming weeks."

The road straddled the Flathead River before ascending into the heart of Glacier Country. Bypassing Going-to-the-Sun Road for now, from the gateway town of West Glacier, they continued east on Highway 2 to East Glacier.

The eastern boundary of Glacier National Park was in the Blackfeet Indian Reservation. The Salish, Kootenai, and Blackfeet Tribes considered this land sacred. It was sacred, an awe-inspiring testament of God's power and majesty.

East Glacier was an offbeat, charming throwback tourist townhospitality, exuding in Native American culture. It was home to the historic Glacier Park Lodge, part of the chain of grand hotels built by the Great Northern Railway in the early 1900s. Amtrak continued to service East Glacier on its Empire Builder line.

Stopping briefly for gas and a snack break, the couple merged onto Montana Highway 49. This sweeping, rambling road followed the eastern edge of the park boundary. The pavement was patched with potholes from the intense snow that tore about the landscape in winter, with high winds from the eastern plains and storms coming off the mountains to the east.

It was a breathtaking sight to twist bends, coming into a panoramic view of vast U-shaped prairies with chiseled glaciated towering mountains in the distance. Though the altitude of the nearby mountain range stood at six thousand to ten thousand feet, the prominence felt gravity-defying. The collision of the Great Plains met the thrust of the Rockies and blended into a high plateau, flat rolling plains with the sheer extreme uplift of the mountains.

Susan and Jake were numbed by the beauty, the drama so intense you couldn't put it into words.

As they turned into the Many Glacier park entrance, the scattered blue sky was eclipsed by a deep fog misting over the mountains. The storm didn't deter them. If anything, the rich atmosphere and mystery of the mountains lured them into exploring the landscape.

Opened by the Great Northern Railway in 1915, the magnificent five-story Many Glacier Hotel was a Swiss chalet–inspired alpine resort, dating to the grand days of railroad tourism. Situated on the eastern shore of Swiftcurrent Lake, the building was a series of chalets, up to four stories tall, offering rustic alpine comfort with an unrivaled view of Chief Mountain.

The elegance and old-world appeal possessed the romantic air of European alpine chalets, with Swiss themed décor. It was fair to say that Glacier was the Switzerland of America. The chiseled peaks, clouds that you could touch, and glaciers bringing you to the heavens.

"Check-in isn't for a few hours." Jake noted the time, just after eleven o'clock.

"Let's grab a bite to eat. If the weather clears up, we can take the boat ride and hike to Grinnell Lake."

The couple dined in the Ptarmigan Dining Room, the Swiss-inspired décor opening up to picture windows offering dramatic views of Swiftcurrent Lake and the surrounding glacial ridges. Scanning the French American–themed menu, Jake ordered the buffalo stroganoff, while Susan kept it light with a grilled chicken salad.

Following the satisfying lunch, they perused the gift shop, picking up postcards and a few souvenirs. Susan purchased *Place Names of Glacier National Park* in addition to the classic *Blackfeet Tales of Glacier National Park*, by James Willard Schultz.

Schultz, a wilderness adventurer who lived among the Blackfeet many years and married into the tribe, fell in love with the history and oral tradition of the people. His knack for storytelling led to many books about his Western experiences, most notably the culture of the Blackfeet and the myth and majesty of Glacier National Park.

While Jake put their souvenirs in the back of the Subaru, Susan purchased tickets for the one-o'clock boat tour, which included a guided hike to Grinnell Lake.

Since 1938 the Glacier Park Boat Company had ferried tourists across the park's resplendent lakes in historic wooden tour boats. The Many Glacier tour departed from the shores of Swiftcurrent Lake.

Evidence of glaciation jutted out in the peaks, with stratified layers carved over thousands of years by the sharp edge cut of shifting ice and erosion. The peaks, a seemingly impenetrable front, cast a spell. The mists hovering over the teeth of the mountain's jaw opened, revealing craggy points that only mountain goats and the tiny pika dared to tread.

Stepping onto the wooden boat, the couple was greeted by an upbeat tour guide and a National Park Service ranger.

"All abroad the *Chief Two Guns*," Kim, a forestry student and boat captain, announced. "Take in the beauty, the valiant mountains, the icy glacial remnants of packed ice continuing the story of the park's geologic past amidst a quickly changing landscape of warming climates. Today you will have the opportunity to experience the Many Glacier scenery from a unique vantage point. We will cruise Swiftcurrent Lake, then we'll disembark across the shore, walking four hundred yards to board our partner boat, *Morning Eagle*. The *Eagle* will ferry you across stunning Lake Josephine. You will have the opportunity to enjoy a guided hike to azure Grinnell Lake, led by Ranger Rick."

Susan and Jake held hands, both entranced by their surroundings.

"The Chief Mountain juts out to 9,080 feet. This focal mountain is a sacred site for Native Americans in the US and Canada. Natives travel to the base of the mountain for sweetgrass ceremonies. The site is critical to the "vision quest." The Chief is truly an iconic image of Glacier." Kim pointed to the square slab of rock, which projected nearly two thousand feet from the prairie floor below.

"Swiftcurrent Lake is traditionally known as Jealous Woman's Lake and Beaver Woman's Lake. Folk legend tells that a young Kootenai Big Knife had twin sisters for wives. They could not be distinguished except for the fact that one wife spoke slowly, and one wife chattered at a rapid pace. Big Knife did not treat them evenhandedly. He gave one wife a beaver skin, but the other he did not. He promised to return with a beaver skin for his other wife the next day. When he did not return immediately, the wives fought. One wife, named Marmot, challenged her sister, Weasel, to swim the length of Swiftcurrent Lake. Whoever swam successfully to shore without drowning would be Big Knife's wife. Marmot drowned in the contest. The wake of the jealous fight left Big Knife and Weasel with nothing but despair."

"Jealousy is a poison dagger." Jake thought aloud.

As the *Chief Two Guns* docked on the southwestern corner of Swiftcurrent Lake, a cow moose meandered out of the nearby woods. At nine hundred pounds, the female moose went into the nearby water and began to swim.

"Moose are adept in the water, able to hold their breath for up to thirty seconds. You will often see a lone moose on the shores of the lake, feeding on plant vegetation. They are beautiful creatures, but they have a reputation to be reclusive, moody, and belligerent. Remember to respect the wildlife in Glacier. Keep your distance so we can keep them wild."

A short walk led tourists to the shores of idyllic Lake Josephine and the *Morning Eagle* boat. The deep blue lake was cradled by the dense forests and peaks.

"Ranger Rick is here to lead you on a gorgeous backcountry hike to Grinnell Lake. It's a little under a mile and relatively flat. The payoff is worth every step." Kim encouraged boaters to take the opportunity to delve into the forest before the return trip.

"Thank goodness the weather cleared up." Susan cast her stare into the piercing blue sky, in awe of the alpine setting. The Lewis Range soared dramatically to touch the sky.

"The scenery is so spectacular that it lifts up your spirit."

Ranger Rick, a fifty-year-old seasoned interpretive ranger, led a group of twenty Explorers through a plank trail surround by lush forest. The trail meandered for roughly a mile before reaching the southeastern corner of Grinnell Lake.

The intrepid view of the opaque lake and backdrop of Grinnell Glacier and Angel Wing Peak brought Susan to her knees. The spell of the mountains overwhelmed the senses. Across the lake, towering falls collapsed over the sheer rock cliff. The silver cord cascade appeared to float from the frozen pack of Grinnell Glacier, catapulting into the lake below.

"George Bird Grinnell, a leading ornithologist and conservationist who founded the Audubon Society, was instrumental in the formation of Glacier as a national park. He is quoted: 'Far away in the northwestern corner of Montana, hidden from view by clustering mountain peaks, lies an unmapped corner—the Crown of the Continent.'

"This wonderland is a place of life, death, and resurrection. Glacier National Park straddles the Continental Divide, and in its partnership with our Canadian neighbor, Waterton National Park, it is the world's first protected International Peace Park. This ecosystem ranges from prairie to tundra and has numerous microclimates and extremes that in concert create a vibrant center of life. The park is home to over one thousand plant species and hundreds of animal species. Except for bison, Glacier has maintained its historic populations. It has hundreds of grizzly bears that are active in the Many Glacier and Saint Mary Lake areas, feeding on the abundant fish and berry supplies.

"Depending on a drop of rain or the course of melting snow, the water flows into the Pacific, Gulf of Mexico, or the Atlantic Ocean," Ranger Rick continued.

"Is that Grinnell Glacier?" a tourist questioned, referring to the massive ice sheet covering the mountain across the lake.

"It is, and behind Grinnell Glacier you can catch a peek of Salamander Glacier. At one point the two were connected, but warming trends have caused both to retreat substantially. The small gem glacier is also visible on nearby Mount Gould," Ranger Rick answered. "Glacier National Park currently has over a dozen glaciers. Unfortunately, climate change is actively warming the area, causing the ecosystem to shift and melting many of our treasured glaciers. In the mid-1800s the park was home to 150 glaciers, now only twenty-five remain. Over thousands of years, glaciers have painstakingly carved this ecosystem. During the last ice age, ten thousand years ago, Glacier National Park was covered in massive sheets of ice. The forces of glaciation chiseled the mountains into jagged ridges and immaculate teeth formations, while the signature U-shaped valleys created sweeping prairie and high plains habitats. It is interesting to note that most of the park at one time was covered by a shallow sea. The melting of the glaciers not only revealed the activity of the glacial period but offers us a window into millions of years into the past."

"Grinnell Lake is so blue; it is an otherworldly turquoise." Susan turned to Ranger Rick.

"The intense color comes from the silt deposits in the bottom of the lake, which drain down from Grinnell Glacier. That coupled with the reflection of the blue sky gives Grinnell and many of Glacier's lakes their vibrant colors."

"How many lakes are in Glacier?" another hiker questioned.

"One hundred and thirty named lakes, plus over seven hundred additional untouched backcountry lakes. Lake McDonald is the largest of the park's lakes," Ranger Rick answered. "The park's lakes are known as glacial lakes. A glacial lake is formed when a glacier erodes the land, melts, and fills the deep hole the erosion created with the melt water. The result—pristine water and extraordinary beauty."

"I love being here with you, in God's country." Susan squeezed Jake's hand.

"The closest I've been to heaven on earth."

Upon their return to the Many Glacier Hotel, Susan and Jake checked into their room and unloaded the car. The appealing rustic room included two queen size beds, a historic letter writing desk, hardwood floors, and wooden paneling.

"This is truly a 'view with a room.'" Susan opened the curtains, revealing a panorama of Swiftcurrent Lake and Mount Gould.

Taking time to unpack, the couple decided to amble down to the shore, where wildlife viewers were peering through telescopic lenses.

"The tiny white specks appearing as pebbles on the mountains are mountain goats." An observer lent Susan and Jake her binoculars.

"They are so adept. How can they possibly maneuver such rugged terrain? Even the kid goats are moseying along." Susan took in the sight. Mountain goats were the symbol of Glacier National Park with their thick white fur, goat beards, and black horns.

"The mountain goat's feet, cloven hooves that spread apart with sharp dewclaws, are ideal for climbing steep, sheer rock slopes and moving across ice. This climbing advantage gives them protection from predators such as bears and mountain lions. In a way they walk confidently in faith, aware of the danger but willing to take their time and trust their ability to maneuver the harshness of the land."

"Adorable is an understatement," Susan admired.

"I read in the park magazine that mountain goats are not related to goats at all but are their own subspecies of the antelope and bovine family. They're categorized in the independent genus oreamnos. In Greek that translates to mountain nymph," Jake informed her.

"Nymph is fitting—they are magic in these mountains, keepers of the stone and wardens of the deep," Susan mused.

"I hope we can see some more goats tomorrow within camera range. It would be awesome to snap some pictures of these living emblems of the park."

For dinner, Jake and Susan picnicked lakeside with sandwiches and ginger beer. They spent the evening relaxing by the fire in the lodge lobby, engrossed in books and each other. It was a peaceful end to a magical day.

Chapter 25

"All aboard." Joe, a seventy-year-old jammer, motioned as Susan and Jake boarded a historic Red Bus in front of the Many Glacier Hotel.

These vintage motor coaches were built by the White Motor Company from 1936. The open-air tops allowed tourists to sit back and enjoy the scenery of Going-to-the-Sun Road while a "jammer" drove the twists and turns. Bus drivers are nicknamed jammers because of the jamming sound the buses used to make with the manual shifting of gears over the mountain passes.

"Get ready for the adventure of a lifetime." Joe signaled the start of the voyage. "Today we will traverse what is arguably one of the most spectacular stretches of highway in America, roaming and rolling through the crest of the Continental Divide through glacier plains, peaks, and the clouds. Get your cameras out. The open-air windows will allow you to take unobstructed photos while I manage the road. The tour will make numerous photo stops along the fifty-two-mile stretch of Going-to-the-Sun Road. Built in 1932 as the only road across the park, Going-to-the-Sun is an engineering feat. It is sculpted in the most precarious and defying of locales, allowing tourists a chance to 'drive into the sun and dwell amongst the clouds.'"

"This is thrilling," Susan and Jake expressed.

From the Many Glacier Hotel, the jammer drove to nearby Saint Mary's Lodge to pick up several additional passengers. Embarking on the Going-to-the-Sun Road, the path began with immaculate Saint Mary Lake on the left, sandwiched by the sheer cliffs of stratified Two Dog Flats on the left.

"On your left, in the backdrop of Saint Mary Lake, is Triple Divide Peak. Here on the Continental Divide, the waters split three ways: to the Pacific, to the Atlantic, and to the Hudson Bay. Triple Divide can be argued as the true crown of the continent, ruling which way the waters flow from Atlantic to Pacific or the Arctic."

Susan meditated on the crossroads of Glacier. She had stood at the precipice questioning which way to go. Fall down, rise up, veer to the security of the road, or ascend new heights. Seeing the drama unfold in the natural world was comforting and insightful. So many changes have taken place in this landscape—harsh and cruel—yet the mastery of God's hand in the living geology only rendered beauty out of the hardship.

"Two Dog Flats is one of the flattest spots in the park. It used to be a shallow sea prior to the ice age. The last glaciers were here roughly twelve thousand years ago. Receding, they carved this landscape, while revealing eons of geologic activity. This area is a favorite spot for wildlife. Dawn and dusk are the best times for spotting bears, elk, moose, and other animals that call the park home."

The bus stopped at the scenic Wild Goose Island overlook. This dramatic view of Saint Mary Lake was one of the most photographed spots in America. In the near distance lay Wild Goose Island. It derived its name from the number of Canada Geese that called the island home. The panorama's spell wasn't that it rivaled other scenic spots along the road, as much as the dramatic shift in color and light that lent itself to optics that sparked the imagination of artists and photographers. It was a spiritual, dramatic, and serene experience.

The bus rolled on to Sunrift Gorge, a roadside creek, where Joe led the group on a brief and easy hike to Baring Falls. The ravishing falls dramatically dropped 250 feet to Sunrift Gorge.

"Glacier is home to over two hundred dazzling waterfalls," Jammer Joe informed the group.

Vocabulary cannot justify the untamed beauty of this place, Susan realized. *Words fail. Every vista carved is from heaven. One struggles to internalize the reality set before them, the mastery and grandeur of this wilderness land.*

The road climbed as the elevation rapidly ascended from the sweeping open land of Two Dog Flats to the deep alpine forests and tundra of the mountains.

"We are approaching the Jackson Glacier, the largest glacier in the park. This is a turning point in the topography of the region, shifting from prairie to an alpine ecosystem."

The dramatic Siyeh Bend was the shift to higher subalpine and forest vegetation. From the roadside turnout, travelers were treated to fantastic views of the vast alpine meadows set against the backdrop of towering Mount Siyeh and Going-to-the-Sun Mountain.

The road continued to rise sharply, weaving hairpin curves as they approached Logan Pass and the Continental Divide.

"This section of road was one of the most arduous challenges on the Going-to-the-Sun Road," Jammer Joe mentioned as the bus drove the East Tunnel, which seemed to come directly out of Piegan Mountain.

"The entire road is an engineering marvel," Susan said to Jake "To scale these mountains and sculpt a byway that blends into the scenery is amazing."

After stopping briefly for photos at Lunch Creek, the group continued on the road, which sharply shifted upward towards Logan Pass and the Continental Divide.

"At an elevation of 6,646 feet, Logan Pass is the highest point on Going-to-the-Sun. We are straddling the Continental Divide." Jammer Joe pulled into the parking lot. Logan Pass greeted over two million visitors a year. Its location on a narrow stretch of road, in the mountains, prompted the park to offer shuttles to and from Logan Pass to ease the flow of parking. "You have an hour to explore the area around Logan Pass. I'll be leading a tour to the Hidden Lake overlook."

Getting out of the bus, Joe pointed out several bighorn sheep hanging out near the visitor center. The graceful creatures were defined by their large curved horns.

Susan immersed herself in the scenery. The wonder of the landscape was so spectacular it didn't seem real. She tried to reconcile such fantastic imagery with reality.

"Lost in your thoughts?" Jake prodded.

"How can you not be swept away in a place such as this, your inhibitions released, fears present, yet empowered by the trepid courage to explore. Breathing in this air, thin and yet so full of life, I want to shout for joy. It's a surreal experience standing atop a mountain. Your feet able to cross the Continental Divide." Susan let her words wander. "I want to jump into the scenery. You wish that time would stop, just for a moment."

The gravity kept their feet stuck to the ground, yet their hearts ran wild. Susan and Jake had never been closer in spirit. They didn't hesitate as they kissed, ever so sweet and quick a caress, standing onthe threshold of that untapped wilderness.

"Be sure to keep your footsteps on the boardwalk. The meadow is a fragile alpine ecosystem. Your steps can harm growth and a myriad of Lfe that relies on the sustainability of this meadow." The tour guide advised.

The hike to the Hidden Lake overlook was one of the most popular in the park. The 1.7-mile boardwalk traversed through a wildflower carpet alpine meadow, where mountain goats were seen an arm's length away sleeping in beds of the cotton-like bear grass that filled the expanse of the valley. Reynolds Mountain and Mount Clement jutted out to the sky, like rocky bear teeth. Hidden Lake was a sparkling emerald body of water tucked under Bearhat Mountain.

"Our next stop is Oberlin Bend. The steep ridges and vegetation make this a perfect haunt for mountain goats. From the viewing platform you'll snag one of the best views of Going-to-the-Sun Road, with the Garden Wall and panorama as far as the border with Canada. In the distance you can even spot Sperry Chalet."

"Sperry Chalet?" Susan inquired.

"It's one of several backcountry chalets that the Great Northern Railway built in the early 1900s. The idea was that to truly experience Glacier, you need to explore the backcountry. Tourists would stay at Many Glacier or other main lodges for a few days before backpacking or riding their horses to remote chalets. Sperry still operates as a backcountry chalet. You can hike in and be greeted with a meal and room, not to mention reclusive scenery."

"Sounds like an adventure worth taking." Jake tugged at Susan's arm.

Continuing on Going-to-the-Sun Road, the Triple Arches, three stone bridges, stood out, another example of the care that engineers put into the nature-inspired design of the road.

"Look at all the roadside waterfalls." Susan's heart raced as a series of trickling cascades carved down the stone wall lining the road.

"This is the Weeping Wall. In the spring and early summer, the force of the water is so strong from melting snow that the falls flood the road at times. It is a mystic and haunting image even in late summer, the Garden Wall tearing up, in awe of the beauty before it."

Jammer Joe stopped the bus at the Bird Woman Falls lookout. At a descent of 560 feet the falls were one of the tallest and certainly among the most dramatic in the park. The falls were visible for two miles along the road at a distance as they spiraled down the cliffs. Even at 560 feet, the falls were a mere shadow to the height of the mountain.

A sharp series of switchbacks defined the Loop, a sharp curve in the road that helped ease the road's elevation gain.

Passing through the West Tunnel, two alcoves exposed a stunning vista of Heaven's Peak.

The tour bus stopped at Avalanche Creek, a popular hiking area and backcountry campsite. Jammer Joe led the group on the Trail of Cedars tour. This short, half-mile roundtrip hike traced its path through an old-growth forest of giant red cedars, hemlock, and cottonwoods.

Glacier is home to the easternmost cedar forest in the west. Rains and moisture moving inland from the coast get trapped in the mountains before reaching the Continental Divide. The rainfall creates an inviting environment for a variety of plant life. Ferns and other shade-loving plants thrive on the forest floor as filtered light penetrates the forest canopy."

Trekking into the thick forest, the scent of ancient cedar and the cool dampness of the air reminded Susan of her time spent in Seattle, when she hiked into the Cascades. She shrugged off the memory of hiking with Bradley in Olympic National Park two summers back.

A trail bridge crossed Avalanche Creek, providing exquisite views of the tumultuous Avalanche Gorge. The deep gorge was defined by fast-moving whitewater, beating down a narrow channel of moss-laden argillite rock. The brunt force of the water thrust through the gorge created a constant mist.

"The forest is so welcoming with vibrant, rich greens." Susan breathed in the fresh air.

"Think of all the stories these trees can tell, their deep roots a foundation for the forest and this ecosystem. They have experienced changes in weather and population, yet still stand strong," Jake mulled.

"My dad always said to live your life like a tree. A tree with a strong foundation, roots planted deeply in hope and love, perseverance, and service, can withstand the fires and floods. Looking at this forest, I think he had it right."

"Kip Blanchard was a wise man."

The Red Bus pulled into the Lake McDonald Lodge parking lot just before two o'clock. First opened in 1914, the Swiss-inspired chalet was designed by famed architect Kirtland

Cutter to compliment the surrounding scenery of Lake McDonald. It faced the eastern shore of the lake, as it was originally accessible only via water.

The three-story, elegant edifice exuded alpine character. The building had a stone foundation with wood framing and white stucco. The exterior of the upper levels was clad in dark brown wooden clapboards, with sawn-in patterns. It was an almost fairy-tale abode with European charm coupled with pastoral ruggedness.

The romantic spell of the alpine structure captivated Susan and Jake as they roamed the lofty, rambling stone and cedar lodge. The grand lobby was a gathering place for travelers to discuss the day's journey by the fireplace. The iron fireplace grill included writing in the Kootenai language, a unique touch to the dynamic cultural history of the area. Balconies offered nooks, ideal for reading and people watching.

The lodge had over a hundred hotel rooms, as well as lakeside cabins. The spacious yet cozy Russell's Fireside Lounge offered views of Lake McDonald, and a gift shop connected to the lobby had a diverse selection of gifts.

The tour was given an hour to explore the Lake McDonald area on their own. After a full day of scaling the mountains, photo ops, and wildlife spotting, the couple was famished.

"Let's grab a late lunch at the lodge, Jake suggested. The restaurant was a pizza and burger joint located within walking distance of the lodge.

"Thank you for carrying me away on this rendezvous. It's the best birthday a girl could ask for."

"I wouldn't trade the past two days for gold or silver. Spending time with you is paradise."

"Who knew that Jake Arnett was such a romantic," Susan teased.

"This is deeper than romance, it's love. For better and for worse you hold my heart."

Surveying the menu, Jake ordered the Bob Marshall, a Montana beef burger with Cajun spices and blue cheese. Susan settled on the Siyeh Bend burger, a third pounder with Swiss cheese and sautéed mushrooms atop a homegrown Wheat Montana bun.

By the time they left, the skies had shifted from the crystal blue flawless expanse to a mystical gray, damp overcast mood. With a light drizzle of rain, they held each other close, walking on the shores of Lake McDonald. Their hearts were stirred by the mist rising above the lake. The clouds hovered, so close it felt as though you could touch the atmosphere of the heavens.

In the distance, thunder rumbled, and a streak of zigzagged lightning appeared to hit the lake. The electricity lit a fire between them. Susan couldn't remember the last time happiness had been so easy and so pure. She clutched Jake's hand tighter for fear she might lose this moment, this second chance.

The Red Bus left Lake McDonald Lodge just before four o'clock. The return trip to Many Glacier followed an alternate route, exiting the park via the gateway town of West Glacier. Following Highway 2 for fifty-five miles, the road traversed the Great Bear Wilderness and was straddled by the Flathead Mountains to the south and the Glacier Park boundary to the north. From East Glacier, the bus veered north on MT 49 through the precipice of the High Plains and Rocky Mountains.

The weather vacillated from wet and misty to bright sunshine. At times rain poured through the sun.

"This day was supernatural…words can't describe." Susan looked into Jake's eyes as they disembarked the bus.

"I have a treat in store for tonight." Jake led her into the Many Glacier Hotel. "A birthday surprise."

"You have gone well above the call of duty as far as a birthday planner," Susan objected.

"Let's just say that this is the icing on the cake." Jake's smile made her weak in the knees. "We have reservations for the famed Many Glacier fondue."

"Chocolate fondue…how can I possibly refuse?"

Susan changed into a casual black wrap dress, while Jake wore khakis and an Oxford shirt. The fondue at Many Glacier followed Swiss—style après meal.

Dining on the decadent chocolate, Jake pulled a jewelry box out of his jacket pocket.

"What's this?"

"The icing on the cake."

Inside the box was the necklace that she had admired from Miller's Jewelry.

"Jake, you really shouldn't have." Susan wept, confused by the gift. It was so thoughtful, yet how could she accept it?

"It's nothing," Jake downplayed. "Just a token of our friendship and love. Happy birthday."

"Oh, Jake." Susan tried to restrain her emotions as Jake clasped the necklace around her neck.

With dusk converging over Many Glacier, the couple walked hand in hand by the shores of Swiftcurrent Lake. Thick clouds stormed the mountains, lightning flashing and thunder roaring.

Suddenly the rain crashed down like a flood. Susan and Jake rushed to get back into the hotel, soaking wet and freezing. Memories of the past, another night like this when the world was at their fingertips, emerged. The night when the rains fell and the storm raged, the night that they nearly sealed their love. Circumstances forced that first chance to drown in the rain, lost, but not forgotten.

Rushing up to the hotel room, the couple struggled with words as the lights flickered from the storm. The air was heavy. They wanted to fall into one another's arms and never let go—still, there was a hesitancy. Neither wanted to rush this, yet with every drop of rain and clap of thunder their love sharpened, and their resolve crashed down. One kiss, so soft.

"I don't want to pressure you…" Jake whispered, caressing her skin. "I love you and will wait until the end of time, if you want me to."

"I love you." Susan kissed Jake. "I'm not ready for…"

"You don't have to explain."

"Just hold me."

Susan and Jake woke up in each other's arms. No lines crossed and yet both fearful that this seemingly perfect happiness would fall apart, taken away from them like summer's last gasp of heat.

As Susan showered, she looked down at the wedding ring she still had on her left hand. She was tempted to remove them but hesitated. It just didn't feel right, even in this moment of reclaimed love, to take them off.

She would keep the ring on her finger until after the local Memorial Service at St. Michaels later that week.

Before checking out of the hotel, the couple grabbed muffins in Heidi's Snack Shop, taking in one last view of the sacred mountains before them. The sun had emerged victorious from last night's storm, blue sky and warmth taking hold of the landscape.

"The lodge is hosting a barn dance this weekend as a final kickoff to the end of summer. It would be wonderful if you would be my date. We can use the event as a chance to announce the obvious, that we are officially a couple," Jake suggested.

"I can't." Susan's tone was unintentionally harsh.

"After last night I thought..." Jake was confused by her outburst.

"I'm sorry. My tone was severe," Susan said. "I have to do something this weekend, something private and personal..."

"You can trust me."

"I have to do something for Bradley."

"Bradley?" Jake didn't disguise his anger.

"It's his birthday and he requested in his will that I schedule a private memorial on the first birthday after his death."

"While you don't owe Bradley anything, it is the Christian thing to do." Jake gulped down his pride.

"I need to do this—it'll be healing."

"You know I'm here for you." Jake kissed Susan on the cheek. "Why don't we go downstairs and have a delicious breakfast. We can go on a hike before we head back to Solitude Lake."

"Sounds perfect."

Chapter 26

Back at the Lone Moose, Susan immersed herself in prepping for the school year. She had been on cloud nine since the trip to Glacier and yet she still had one difficult task—going through a box of Bradley's papers that she'd received in the mail last month from the attorney.

She wondered if this box held the answers to all the deception and pain. As desperately as she longed to uncover the motivation behind his duplicity, she was in a place of peace now and unmotivated to kick up dust.

She ignored the boxes for now, she had enough baggage of her own to sort out the aftershocks of Bradley's mistakes. The relationship had been divided with a cracked foundation. He was dead and her decision to forgive and let go of the bitterness was the only way she could stitch up the threads of love to a point that she could be at peace. Giving up the anger thread by thread, stitch by pain-wrenching stitch.

Bradley's memorial service had been healing. Father Leo said a memorial Mass for Bradley's soul and they planted flowers in his honor in the church garden.

"Bradley's funeral was months ago, and yet I never really felt as though I buried him," Susan told Father Leo. "The funeral home sent his ashes here right after his death and you offered a private Mass, but it didn't feel official."

"Burying the dead can bring closure, but it doesn't end our grieving. The best way to truly let the dead rest in peace is for us to keep on living," Father Leo handed Susan a handkerchief as tears fell like a cleansing rain. "Jesus holds Bradley in his arms now. Take courage. Things will get easier."

For the first time since Bradley's death, she sat by the columbarium wall and mourned Bradley's remains – screaming out her hurt and releasing her pain in a breath of deep forgiveness. Bradley hurt her and she was entitled to that hurt, but holding onto the rage would only infect her with bitterness. The sort of wound Bradley carried. The impact of his father's rejection had left him scarred. Bradley for all his faults, was a good man. Like all humans he carried crosses and fought sin.

"I forgive you Bradley. It hurts like hell, but I pray you are finally at peace."

Ellis Dixon was a no-show. Susan made peace with the fact that Bradley's father was unchangeable. God would have to deal with Ellis; he wasn't Susan's problem to worry about.

After catching up on work, Susan curled up on the couch with her daily devotional lesson. Today's focus was on Psalm 18, verses 6 and 17:

"In my distress I called upon the LORD, and cried unto my God: he heard my voice out of his temple, and my cry came before him, even into his ears. Then the earth shook and I trembled; the foundations also of the hills moved and were shaken because of his wroth."

The verses resonated with Susan, who jotted her reflections in her journal.

Throughout time, people have struggled to stand—under the façade of pride they are frail and afraid. The psalmist cry for help coupled with the lament of anguish displayed the raw conflict of crisis and grief. You are unable to understand how God, all loving and all encompassing, could allow you to be surrounded by wolves, left to fend for your flesh. Yet in that despair, you cry out to God, with the humble confidence of hope. In the darkness, the worst weakness and fear that you need the light of God's mercy and help to guide. The more we try to avoid God, the more we need his compassion and love. We long for his healing. He never forsakes us. We may be tested by fire, but he will not let us burn if we cry out. God hears our cries for help and longs to console us. God listens and answers our prayers. We must be willing to cast aside our fear and pride and learn to listen and to trust, even if we don't like the response we may receive in prayer. Trust that though he may ask us to climb mountains he will never push us off a cliff, but instead lift us out of troubled waters.

Her silent contemplation was brashly interrupted by pounding on the front door. Startled by the aggressive knocks, she hesitated before answering.

"Damn well took you long enough." The gruff, callous voice pricked at Susan's spine. In a state of motionless shock, she scrambled to speak.

"Ellis…"

"That is Mr. Dixon to you, Ms. Blanchard." The imposing six-foot, 240-pound seventy-one-year-old forced himself inside the cabin.

"If I had known that you were coming…" Susan's mind raced at a confused pace. For months she had reached out to Bradley's father, begging to make peace. Her letters requesting his presence at the prayer service had been systematically returned, without the courtesy of explanation. She questioned his motives for showing up unannounced.

"Still such a fragile creature." Ellis scrutinized Susan. "Then again, Bradley always pursued lost causes."

"Why are you here, Ellis?" Susan mustered the strength to offer fighting words. Even after the death of his son, Ellis appeared unaffected by grief and remorse. He acted like the same acerbic, narrow-minded bully that had stepped into Hidden Creek two decades ago.

"You've barraged me with letters the past eight months. I saw the correspondence as an open invitation," Ellis scoffed.

"You never had the decency to offer a reply," Susan shot back.

"Why waste ink with what needs to be said face-to-face." Ellis's dark eyes examined the widow. Susan's expression was bold and apprehensive. She was aware of how violent her father-in-law could be. "Sit down and let's get to business."

Reluctantly, Susan sat down.

"Sorry you missed the memorial Mass. I hoped that you'd join me at the church in celebrating the life of your only son."

"I must say that I am surprised. That after the hell Bradley put you through, you can stand in a church and pray for him."

"Do you have no respect for your flesh and blood? He loved you and desperately wanted your love. Instead, you spent your life antagonizing him. He always felt cast out in your shadow."

"I would have given the world to my son, but he made the critical mistake of rebelling against me. He betrayed me and I cut him out. Simple as that."

"You betrayed Bradley by being a horrible father, domineering and selfish, cruel and abusive. Yet, in spite of your weakness and hate, he still loved you. I think you owe it to your son to step up and remember him with dignity and love. Make peace—if not for your sake, then for the son who you lost. Mourn for him in love, not bitter anger. Put aside your ego for the sake of your child."

"Bradley only pursued you to rebel against me. I taught him to be defiant, bitter, and to fight. I just never thought he'd turn on me. To side with my adversary, your leech of a father, was bad enough. Bradley loved seeing me squirm. Frankly, I encouraged his rebellion. If my son wanted a shot in hell of getting ahead in life, he damn well needed to cut some skin and bleed out a little. I knew that he was his father's son when he married you. It was a calculated move, the stake through the heart to shove me into a corner. He knew that nothing would make me sweat blood more than his marrying the daughter of a man that I loathed. The man who ruined my reputation and forced me to the forsaken badlands of Glendive on a shoddy oil deal."

"If you think that Bradley only married me as some sort of twisted game to get back at you, you're wrong," Susan objected, secretly afraid that Ellis was telling the truth.

"That is exactly why he married you. Heck, he wouldn't even marry you in a proper church. He manipulated you into a quick elopement, a romantic entanglement, where it was you against the world."

"You have a flawed memory."

"Do I?" Ellis laughed. "The funny thing is that I was thrilled that he married you. A reliable, smart, and sensitive girl that was just pretty enough to prevent him from getting into trouble. I only let my son think that I was against the marriage. The thing is, a successful man needs to have a chip on his shoulder to rise to new heights. I wanted Bradley to hate me because that hate was fueled by the desire to please me and in pleasing me, then he would rise to fortune and success. Having you as his wife was a constant reminder that he had to work hard to please me, because he'd married a girl that I claimed to despise."

"You are a sick piece of work."

"Everything that I did for him was out of love."

"It isn't love; it is and always was about control and contrived games." Susan flared. "Your hurtful behavior might have wounded Bradley, but he did not succumb to the hate and wickedness that dwells in your soul. Bradley was flawed, but he loved me."

"My son was a tyrant who lied to you. He stole hundreds of thousands of dollars from your pension to pay off gambling debts," Ellis said, trying to antagonize her.

"I want you to leave," Susan demanded.

"I'll leave, after we finish our business."

"What business do you have here if not to pray for the memory of your son and uphold his honor? I have nothing to say to you."

"I have a few more things to say to you." Ellis's tone thawed. "Did I screw up my son's life? Perhaps. He managed to mess up things on his own. He came to me, desperate and humiliated after the losses with his company. I could tell that he had started gambling. He was presenting his case like a dealer who wanted to pick me apart. He begged me for cash to pay his debts. I agreed on one condition. I told Bradley that I would not only pay his debts but also pay out a hefty inheritance—money I'd pilfered from his mother before we divorced—if he agreed to divorce you."

"You hate me that much?"

"No. I liked you well enough that I thought you deserved better than my lying reckless son. A divorce would have been a much better option. You wouldn't have lost your retirement and Bradley would be able to stand on his own two feet with the threat of loan sharks gnawing at his back."

"What did Bradley say?"

"Point-blank, he refused my offer. He said that he loved you beyond life itself and would rather die than give you up. I admonished him for being selfish, subjecting you to a life of poverty. He cried. He said that your love was the only thing that kept his heart beating and if I took you away from him that his life would have no meaning. He said that you would forgive him, and he would make up the losses somehow. This occurred three weeks before he died. It turns out that in the end my son wasn't pretending. He loved you."

A long and uneasy lapse in conversation stiffened the air. Susan wrangled with a thousand emotions—hurt, misunderstanding, love, hate, disregard, and forgiveness. The insight was alarming, comforting, and cruel all at the same time.

"I would have forgiven Bradley...I am in the process of forgiving him. Our love was never based on material things. The secrets he died with broke me up inside. I wanted honesty. Had he lived, I don't doubt that we could have sorted this out. I certainly would not have forsaken our love simply to receive a payout from you. Yes, there would have been a broken trust, but love heals scattered hearts."

"I will not be attending Bradley's second memorial tomorrow. You deserve the privacy to mourn him in peace. I did think it was fair to shed some insight, even if it was bleak, into the situation." Ellis stood up, preparing to leave. "In this envelope you'll find a letter from Bradley. He wrote it to me hours before he passed away. Probably dropped it in the mail minutes before his accident."

"Goodbye, Ellis." Susan brushed aside tears as she forced him out of the cabin. She didn't want to give him the satisfaction of seeing her cry.

"I recommend that you stop by your bank.In that envelope there is a certified check in your name, waiting to be deposited. You have my sympathy and regret."

"I don't want your sympathy and I certainly don't want your money," Susan railed.

"It isn't my money. The cash is a trust, squirreled away for Bradley. I wouldn't dare give a cent of my own money away, definitely not to a Blanchard."

With that Ellis drove away, leaving a pile of dust flying, nearly blinding Susan. The air heavy as a hammer on a nail, her head ached with confusion. All the bent-up anger and grief, forgiveness and mercy, erupted in a storm, her sky a murky gray releasing all emotions with hurricane force.

Chapter 27

Susan arose from a listless sleep, her mind wrapped in a web of questions. Her soul was conflicted by varying degrees of logic, angst, hope, and unstable understanding. For months she had anxiously obsessed over the motivation behind Bradley's recklessness. She'd grieved, languishing on how he could betray her trust. The admission from Ellis Dixon that Bradley had forgone financial assistance from his father to stay married to Susan was heartrending. It tore into her psyche. Bradley had loved Susan. That much was not a lie.

Beneath that love was a complicated relationship. Call it a paradox, an irony of sorts. It was so convoluted Susan couldn't quite pinpoint the nucleus. Bradley's twisted relationship with his father had turned him inside out. Susan had no doubt that his gambling and folly had been rooted in the psyche of a dysfunctional relationship with his father. Still, Bradley had acted by his own volition, making horrible mistakes, and refusing to be honest with his wife.

Susan teetered between the aha moment of "yes, my husband loved me" to sharp rage at the selfishness that he hadn't come to her directly about his debt, in the process stealing her pension funds. It was selflessness and selfishness at the same time. A jarring multilateral spiral of the will to do the right thing while reverting to self-seeking aims.

Bradley knew that Susan loved him undeterred by reason. Strong and independent as she was, Susan would have forgiven his plundering if he had just been honest and up-front with her about the finances. Yes, the trust would have been fractured. There would have been consequences. Bradley's actions merited consequences, but she would have been willing to listen and to have compassion if he had been honest with her.

The fact that Bradley went to Ellis Dixon to ask for money showed how desperate he was for the cash. Did he want to remedy the situation for himself or out of love for his wife? Did he feel remorse for stealing her money, their future retirement, or was he anxious to get debtors off his back while also getting the next round of cash to continue his gambling? Even then Susan's love would have given him a chance for redemption and to rebuild that trust.

Bradley swore to his father that he would never give Susan up. Were his actions motivated out of love or something far more selfish? Did he view his wife as a possession of sorts, a crutch? *Love.* Susan pondered the word. She questioned a love that was intertwined with deception. One could argue it was sacrifice. The lines were blurred. For the first time in months everything was muddy.

Dragging herself out of bed and into the kitchen, she spotted the envelope Ellis Dixon had given her the day before. Pride told her to tear up the check inside. It was the principle of the matter. But anger and reason told her that she was entitled to the money. Awareness reminded Susan she was in no position to turn the financial bequest down.

She thought about the letter. If Bradley had time to ask his father for financial assistance and write him a letter, then he could have had the courtesy to fill her in about the train wrecking in their lives. This duplicity had gone on for years. She could argue that had he lived he would have told her the truth, he would have been forced to. Instead, he died, his voice silent, and she was left with *why?*

Susan decided to forgive Bradley – a decision of the mind, even if the heart was slow to forgive. Forgiveness was her only option. Allowing lingering questions to rattle her mind wouldn't lead to peace. Susan needed to let it go.

Susan debated whether to tell Jake about Ellis's visit. The encounter remained raw, but better to be open with him.

"How's my favorite girl?" Jake picked Susan up for lunch. On the drive into Hidden Creek, Susan was silent and pale as a ghost, her eyes red from dried tears.

"Are you okay?" Jake said gently.

"Ellis Dixon stopped by the cabin yesterday." Susan released her frustration as they entered the Timber's Edge.

"I'm so sorry." Jake squeezed her hand.

"He is a malicious man. The vehement things he said to me…"

Susan went on to describe her encounter with Ellis Dixon in painstaking detail. "Bradley chose to forgo money to rectify his fiscal bankruptcy to stay married to me. I never would have simply divorced him because of finances—not if he was truly of a contrite heart and wanted to rectify and mend the brokenness in the relationship. I question if his motivations in refusing his father's terms were based on love or selfishness."

"I don't think you want my opinion," Jake said, trying to control his anger at the Dixon men. How dare Ellis treat Susan so deplorably. And Bradley—he was no victim and yet Jake still felt pity for the deceased.

Susan respected Jake's silence. Words didn't need to be spoken. She could understand his thoughts by looking into his eyes.

"Should I cash the check?"

"Yes," Jake said firmly. "That money is yours and you are not tied in any way to Ellis Dixon. Of course, I respect your decision…my stubborn pride would probably tear up that check, but it's not rational."

"Thanks for listening, Jake." Susan managed a smile.

"I love you, Susan. You don't have to go through this alone." Jake wanted to keep her safe—but he knew he couldn't heal the wounds Bradley left. He could hopefully rebuild her future, though.

Chapter 28

Summer refused to give up its ghost. September was less than a week away. Susan wasn't ready for the chill of fall and winter, and yet she knew it was coming.

"You free for a day trip to Wild Horse Island tomorrow," Jake called Susan. She'd spent the day prepping her classroom for the upcoming schoolyear. "I know you're off and I asked Gil to cover me."

"I'm always up for a trip to Flathead Lake," Susan agreed.

"I'll pick you up at seven a.m."

"I'll have the coffee ready."

"Fresh-roasted coffee in the thermos and a cooler with lunch goodies," Susan noted as she got in Jake's car.

Flathead Lake was roughly an hour north of Hidden Creek. Spanning 197 square miles, the glacial lake was the largest freshwater body of water west of the Mississippi; it had a fathomless depth of 370 feet, deeper than the Yellow Sea and Persian Gulf. The lake beckoned travelers from all over the world to dip their toes into the translucent waters.

Susan let her mind wander as she lost herself in the sheer majesty of the vast lake. Her soul was captured by the deep waters and miles of lonely shoreline, set against the backdrop of the Salish and Mission Mountain ranges jolting into the big sky. Staring into the mystery and magic of the scenery, Susan struggled to reconcile the upheaval she'd faced since May. The dramatic shift of a fractured winter to the ease of a late-summer day on the first Saturday in September juxtaposed against love and loss, heartache, and repair.

The past week had straddled the awkward shift between stages in the seasons in one's life. It seemed like just yesterday that Susan drove down the gravel road to the Lone Moose, broken and scarred, nearly destitute and without hope... Funny how in barely four months her world turned upside down, from her job at the lodge, to her romance with Jake, and now she was prepping to transition into her teaching job at Hidden Creek High. The whirlwind of time and motion grabbed her like a twister on a wild horse running into the horizon.

At 2,163 acres, Wild Horse Island was the largest island on Flathead Lake—. Its name was derived from the small, elusive, yet hearty population of wild horses that call the island home.

Salish Kootenai natives used the island as a pasture for their horses to prevent them from being stolen by other tribes. In addition to the horse population, the park was known as a sanctuary for population of bighorn sheep, mule deer, songbirds, waterfowl, bald eagles, and falcons. Wild Horse Island was a true unbridled, mystical land where life was still wild.

They departed Bigfork's Marina Cay just after nine o'clock on one of the several lake cruisers for rent. The catamaran buzzed as the sound of the wake of the calm waters soothed Susan's mind.

"How many horses are on the island?" Susan asked the boat captain as they skimmed the surface of the lake's unfathomable deep.

"Five as of last count. That's the maximum number of horses allowed on the island to ensure that there's ample foraging for healthy populations. We lost Old Gelding last spring. He roamed this island home for more than three decades, at one point as the lone equine resident, until FWP transferred additional wild horses onto the island."

"Old Gelding. He was a fiery old horse that would protect the fillies on the island, snorting at tourists who threatened their safety. He had a personality that was tenacious and endearing."

"Every winter, his ribs were more pronounced and his winter coat tattered and flimsy—everyone expected the old man to die, but he always fought back. He braved the forces of winter, island predators such as coyotes and mountain lions, the weakness of the flesh. He finally succumbed to greener pastures. You cannot live forever, but that old man, give him credit for living life to the fullest while he lived these wilderness years."

Docking on the island's Skeeko Bay just after ten o'clock, Susan and Jake stepped onto the rocky expanse of shore, where the island's wonderland awaited.

"See you kids back here at four o'clock sharp." Chuck pointed at his wristwatch. "Don't make me send out a search party."

Grabbing their packs, the couple crossed the driftwood-scattered beach, heading up into the island's open forest and prairie environment. Before embarking on the trailhead, into the heart of the island, Jake and Susan sat on a log and ate lunch.

Neither said much in between sandwich bites, both lost in their own thoughts, happy with each other's presence.

Susan snapped several shots of the unobstructed view of Flathead Lake before delving into the island's splendid mystery. Less than three miles of trails left most of this island untouched by human steps. The 2,163 acres were defined by rolling Palouse Prairie, glacier carved ridges, and trees that rose high above the mighty inland "sea" of Flathead Lake.

True to its promise, the island was wild and beautiful. Twenty minutes into the hike, a herd of nearly forty bighorn sheep appeared rambling, hoofs against the prairie floor. The power and serenity of that moment captured in a picture, etched in memory. Shortly thereafter a group of mule deer hopped across the trail.

"Their high bouncing gait allows them to jump as far as fifteen feet high and two feet across," Jake noted. He had so many things he wanted to ask Susan, about Bradley and about the future of their relationship, yet the day was too pure to taint it with doubt.

As they neared Eagle Cove, a sleek, elegant, unrefined black horse sprang through the adjacent meadow, with an untamed neigh.

"Look at all the pretty horses," Susan whispered, grasping Jake's shoulder as the five equine residents galloped blissfully.

The horses stopped ten yards ahead of the pair, grazing and grooming each other. The horses did not seem bothered by the onlookers, even posing for a picture. Still, Jake and Susan respected their wildness. Some things are so beautiful that you desire their touch, yet the true beauty lies in keeping one's distance.

They reached Skeeko Bay just after three o'clock. Finding a spot on the shore, the couple sat on a large piece of driftwood.

"I know I'll never fully be over Bradley's death. The pain will linger," Susan surmised. "Yet being here with you—in this last flash of summer—I know it's all going to be okay. I can forgive my mistakes, Bradley's transgressions, and let it roll away with the tide of the lake."

"I'm sorry I hurt you years ago, Susan. I used to pity myself and was so stubborn—thinking it was your fault for leaving—but I know I let you down."

"The past is the past." Susan threw a pebble into the water. "Let's focus on the future now."

Chapter 29

The lodge's Labor Day cookout was the unofficial sendoff to the summer season in Hidden Creek. The town gathered for a huge barbeque and potluck with live music and fireworks.

It seemed like the perfect time for Susan and Jake to officially announce their relationship, although Molly disagreed when Jake threw a proposal into the mix.

"Mom, I want to ask Susan to marry me."

"Marriage? Don't be ridiculous," Molly said, dismissive. "You just reconnected, and Susan's barely buried her husband."

"Why are you so bitter towards Susan? I'm the one who let her go years ago."

"I don't question the fact you love one another, but it is a tangled love. Give it time. You don't need to rush into anything."

"I've waited over fifteen years to ask Susan to marry me. It's not rushing into anything."

"Do you think she'll say yes?" Molly could see the pain Susan still carried. In time she would be the perfect daughter-in-law, but right now Susan needed to heal.

"Only one way to find out." Jake was confident. "I want to propose with Grandmother's sapphire ring."

"I don't know, dating is one thing, but…proposing…it's a lot."

"Mom, let me make my own decisions. If I crash and burn, that's on me."

"Of course you can have Grandmother's ring." Molly sighed. "Just remember you only have one heart."

"Thanks, Mom, I love you." Jake understood his mom's point of view, but if he was going to risk his heart, it would always be on Susan.

"Don't propose to her over beans and BBQ. Be romantic." Molly's expression softened. The Arnett matriarch was reconciled to Jake and Susan's relationship…but she wanted to make sure Susan's intentions were on the same page as Jake's.

"Give me some credit, Mom," Jake kidded. "You raised me after all."

Susan was in the middle of prepping her classroom at Hidden Creek High School for the fall term when she received a call from Molly Arnett.

"Susan, I need to speak with you."

"Is everything okay?" Susan sensed the urgency in Molly's voice.

"I need to discuss something personal with you. Can we meet at the Lone Moose when you finish up at the high school?"

"I'll be home in forty-five minutes."

Susan hung up, perplexed by the call. Molly wouldn't have reached out unless it was important.

"I'm finished here," Susan said, stacking the final set of textbooks on the classroom shelves. "I better get home."

"Thank you for meeting me on such short notice." Molly stepped into the Lone Moose.

"Of course." Susan offered her guest a glass of water. "What's going on?"

"I've never been one to beat around the bush, so I'll get straight to the point... Jake is in love with you, and I want to know how you feel about Jake...not just for today, but forever. Are you serious about him or is this just a rebound romance for you?"

The question caught Susan off guard. She remained silent for several minutes, pondering the question in her heart. She too had battled the question so many times in the past few months. As much as Susan wanted to close her heart and just write her feelings for Jake off as sentimental, she knew that was a lie. Susan had always loved Jake. That didn't mean she hadn't loved Bradley, but it was a different love. She couldn't carry that love as if it were alive now. It would remain with her—Bradley always would be part of Susan—but her future belonged to Jake Arnett.

"I love Jake. I always have."

"Yet you married Bradley and broke Jake's heart." Molly paused. "At least that is what I believed for the past fifteen years. I blamed you, Susan, for hurting Jake, but he hurt you too. He wasn't honest with his feelings. Jake broke your heart and I understand why you married Bradley. I'm sorry."

"It's not your fault," Susan followed. "I love Jake and a part of me wishes I could go back in time—not elope with Bradley—but that isn't possible. Honestly, I know God had a plan and Bradley was part of the story. I do love Bradley and always will, but that doesn't mean I don't love Jake. Bradley is my past. Jake is my future."

"That's all I needed to hear." Molly embraced Susan. The bitterness of the past gone...the future wide open.

Chapter 30

"I can't believe school starts on Tuesday," Marjorie said as they prepared Hidden Creek High's open house. The school was small—only one hundred students—but what it lacked in size it made up in heart. The educational community was strong and Hidden Creek consistently ranked among the top schools in the northwest.

"I'm excited, but nervous," Susan said. said.

"Don't overthink it, you are going to do great," Marjorie encouraged.

The open house welcomed students to meet with their new teachers and reconnect with classmates. While Susan was a familiar face to many students, she enjoyed the ability to speak with her future classes one on one.

"We have an exciting year ahead. Literature and history are full of drama and excitement. I promise this isn't going to be your run-of-the-mill class—we are going to travel the world without leaving Hidden Creek, from Rome to London and beyond. You'll be taken to faraway lands, from Narnia to nineteenth-century

London to the ruins of Greece." Susan's passion shone through. Her students were energized to start the year.

After the open house, Marjorie pulled the staff into a quick meeting. They recapped the itinerary for the following week, before Marjorie brought up a pressing topic.

"Unfortunately, we're having to scale back some of our audiovisual and computer courses due to some unexpected budget changes. A key grant is being postponed." Marjorie explained the situation. "Our town's community is strong, and I'm hoping that we can organize a fundraiser of sorts to help shoulder the costs."

"We could set up a fall festival." Macy Wilcox, the algebra teacher spoke up. "Sell raffle tickets."

"I'm sure local vendors would donate some prizes." The staff agreed. "We can get publicity in local papers."

"Anyone up for the challenge to head the committee?" Marjorie asked.

Everyone jumped at the chance to donate their time for the school.

"I would love to help plan the event," Susan said, stepping up. "I actually can donate something of value for the fundraiser."

"I'm all ears." Marjorie was curious, aware of the issues Susan had faced since Bradley's death.

"I have a first-edition copy of Charles Dickens's *Great Expectations*." Susan explained the story of the book to Marjorie. "I've been hanging on to it, but it's time for the book to have a new beginning. I want to auction it off for the fundraiser."

"That is too generous," Marjorie said, overwhelmed with gratitude.

"I don't know if it'll bring in tons of money, but at least it will bring some publicity and hopefully help the program."

"You are a lifesaver, Susan. I have 'great expectations' of your future at HCHS."

Before heading home, Susan stopped by Marmot Books and Coffee for a caffeine fix.

"Howdy, stranger." Lacy embraced her friend. "Can I interest you in a Flathead Cherry Latte."

"Sounds delicious, but I'll stick with my old summer standby—Huckleberry Vanilla," Susan decided.

"How are things going?" Lacy inquired. "I've only heard amazing things about the summer program you created at the lodge."

"It was fun." Susan paused to sip her coffee.

"And you and Jake seem to be falling into each other's arms again." Lacy had known Susan and Jake since youth, but even a blind eagle could see the attraction and care they had for one another.

"Lacy, I think you've been reading too much Jane Austen," Susan teased. "But yes, Jake and I are enjoying spending time together."

"I'm glad to see you smiling again."

"I'm in need of a new page turner—any suggestions?"

"I've got just the book…" Lacy handed Susan a copy of the new Kate Morton, a favorite author of the pair.

"Hi, Susan." Father Leo popped into the store. "Ready for the school year?"

"I'm excited for the adventure."

"I ran into Jake Arnett." Father Leo and Susan had spoken in private about her relationship with Jake. Father Leo had given her good advice about not rushing into anything, but also being open to love.

"We're eating dinner at the lodge later," Susan said, making conversation.

"I know you have a lot of emotions on the table, but Jake is a great guy. Don't be afraid to trust again."

"Okay." Susan laughed. Father Leo always had a knowingly calming presence. "I'll remember that."

Across town, Jake was at Yogo Jewelry, his hands shaking as he handed Miller McCloud his grandmother's sapphire ring.

"I need this resized."

"Susan wears a size eight if I recall." Miller grinned.

"Am I that obvious?"

"You both deserve all the happiness in the world." Miller hoped Susan would be smart enough to say "yes" to Jake. He knew they would be very happy together.

"I'd like an inscription…it's from one of her favorite books." Jake handed Miller a piece of paper. "'You are in every line I have ever read.'"

"From Dickens?" Miller knew his literature. "She'll love it."

"When will it be ready for pickup."

"When do you plan to propose?"

"This weekend, after the Labor Day dance at the lodge."

"I'll have it ready tomorrow." Miller smiled. Hopefully this would lead to a happy ending.

"Mom says you plan to propose to Susan." Keeley squealed. "I'm so happy for you."

"Hopefully I can ask Susan first before the gossip mill tells her." Jake rolled his eyes in annoyance.

"Your secret is safe. I just wanted to see if I could help. Make the proposal special?"

"You could help me set a few things up." Jake shared his plan with Keeley.

"Wow, you are the romantic." Keeley hoped Susan wouldn't let fear block her from saying "yes."

Chapter 31

Susan sat on the dock at the Lone Moose, enjoying the crystal-clear waters of Solitude Lake and the Swans in the distance. A fresh layer of snow fell on the peaks. For the first time all summer, Susan wasn't afraid of the changing of the seasons. She had hope for the future—the unknown didn't scare her.

Susan thought about Molly's visit. She pondered her future with Jake. It had all happened so fast and yet they had a lifetime of history.

Digging into her devotional, she meditated on the calming words of Psalm 34:4. "I sought the Lord and he answered me. He delivered me from all my fears."

Susan enjoyed the sunshine until just after 4 p.m. She needed to get ready for the lodge festivities. Jake had said he had a surprise for her. She let go of curiosity. Time would reveal Jake's surprise—right now she enjoyed the moments of solitude by the lake.

Digging into her closet, Susan debated what to wear for the Labor Day weekend dance. She settled on a denim chambray dress with hand-embroidered beadwork. She paired it with her cowgirl boots and her necklace from Jake. It fit the Western flair for the evening.

Susan arrived at the lodge just after six. The band was just starting to warm up, while the smell of brisket and Molly's famed cornbread casserole filled the air.

"You look gorgeous." Jake pulled Susan into his arms.

"You dress up nice too." Susan kissed him. "I'm eager for this surprise of yours."

"Patience is a virtue." Jake was trying to hide his nerves. "Let's grab some dinner."

After sitting down with more food than they'd ever eat, Susan and Jake chatted with the lodge crew.

"The lodge will run on a skeleton crew the rest of the season," Russ noted. "We'll be closed by the end of October."

"We've been entertaining the idea of a winter season—for snowmobilers and skiers," Gilligan added. "We'll decide by next week."

"It seems like a good idea," Susan mused. "Christmas at Solitude Lake sounds wonderful."

After dinner the crowds began to dance to the sounds of several local bands.

"May I have this dance?" Jake took Susan's hand as the band played their favorite song: "The Keeper of my Heart."

"Every last dance." Susan smiled.

As the sunset began to fall into night, Jake signaled Keeley.

"It's time," he whispered to his sister.

"Go get her."

"Ready for my surprise?" Jake squeezed Susan's hand.

"You don't have to do anything special; you know." Susan looked into his eyes. "You already stole my heart."

"Trust me." Jake led Susan away from the crowds to their favorite secluded spot by the lake. The stars were bursting above, the Milky Way's band visible.

"I love the lake at night—stargazing. You don't see this in Seattle."

"The only star I see is you." Jake held her.

Susan smiled. Jake was sentimental, but genuine.

"You're my North Star too," Susan whispered in his ear.

Jake led Susan to a table by the lake with roses and her favorite wine. Keeley had arranged the bouquet and helped mark the path with lantern light.

"What in the world?" Susan exclaimed as she sat down at the table.

"Years ago, Susan, you asked me if I loved you—right here. I was afraid to admit my feelings and I let you go. I know I can't make that up to you, but I hope we can start again."

"We already have." Susan smiled warmly. "The past is the past. I don't regret it. I've had a good life, and you and I are going to create a better future. God's timing is perfect." Susan's words unintentionally forecasted Jake's next move.

"Speaking of the future… I want to spend the rest of my life loving you and being with you, Susan. You are my best friend, my companion and soul mate. I understand you're still mourning the loss of Bradley. I can't replace him, but I hope you'll give me the chance to spend forever with you." Jake knelt, revealing the sapphire engagement ring. "Susan, will you marry me?"

Susan's heart knew the risk. Rationally this was going too fast, but time had seasons, and she knew it was time to let go of the past. She would always love Bradley despite the betrayal, but Jake was her future.

"Yes." Susan's heart leapt.

"I promise I'll do everything in my power to make you happy."

The pair fell into a long and perfect kiss.

"Should we share our news?" Susan was ready to proclaim her love as they returned to the dance. All the disrepair in their hearts was on the mend, the future an open map—their love and friendship would guide them forward.

"I can't wait to start forever with you." Jake held her close, the future brighter than all the stars in the galaxy.

Molly couldn't help but smile seeing the pair together.

"Looks like we'll be planning a wedding." She looked at her husband.

"I can't think of a more perfect ending to the summer," Walt toasted.

About the Author

Adele Darcy is the alter-ego of creative artist, blogger and sales aficionado, Adele Lassiter.

Solitude Lake is inspired by Adele's time living in western Montana, where she spent countless hours exploring Big Sky's wide-open spaces from Glacier National Park to Yellowstone Country and beyond.

She currently resides in North Carolina.

Follow her adventures online:

Short Stories and Art: https://www.adelelassitercreative.com
Travel Blog: https://www.adelelassiter.com
Facebook Page: https://www.facebook.com/ArtisticAdele